1.99

A Pay-off
in Switzerland

By Noah Webster:

A PAY-OFF IN SWITZERLAND
A WITCHDANCE IN BAVARIA
A BURIAL IN PORTUGAL
A KILLING IN MALTA
FLICKERING DEATH

A Pay-off
in Switzerland

NOAH WEBSTER

PUBLISHED FOR THE CRIME CLUB BY

DOUBLEDAY & COMPANY, INC.

GARDEN CITY, NEW YORK

1977

All of the characters in this book
are fictitious, and any resemblance
to actual persons, living or dead,
is purely coincidental.

Library of Congress Cataloging in Publication Data

Knox, Bill, 1928–
A pay-off in Switzerland.

I. Title.
PZ4.K748Pay 1977 [PR6061.N6] 823'.9'14
ISBN: 0-385-13246-8
Library of Congress Catalog Card Number 77-74271

For Bill Morris

A Pay-off
in Switzerland

"Para 40. The Treasury in practise delegate to the Queen's and Lord Treasurer's Remembrancer the powers conferred on them by paragraph (4) of section 37 of the Exchange Control Act, 1947, to give directions to persons . . . suspected of contraventions of the Act."

CHAPTER 1

Jonathan Gaunt watched, fascinated. Beside him, the thin fair-haired mechanic rested one hand on the loudly throbbing engine being bench-tested, eyes almost closed, a look of concentration on his narrow, unshaven face.

Their surroundings weren't impressive. The old hut was grimy and dilapidated, with one cracked window which looked out on the sluggish green water of a canal with some of Edinburgh's worst tenement property on the other side. But that was incidental.

The mechanic's name was Dan Cafflin. He was deaf and dumb, he worked on his own, and turned away business when he felt he'd rather go fishing—which was often. Yet Gaunt knew him to be probably the best car tuner in the Scottish capital. Engines spoke to Dan Cafflin through his sensitive fingertips, each vibration carrying an individual message.

And the engine being tested belonged to Jonathan Gaunt's newest pride and joy, the small dark red Chrysler lying waiting at the other end of the hut. He watched Cafflin for another few moments then turned to the third man in the hut, a bulky, business-suited figure who had only just arrived.

"Hear the difference, Henry?" he asked enthusiastically.

Henry Falconer, senior administrative assistant to the

Queen's and Lord Treasurer's Remembrancer, the mediaeval title still used by the head of one of Scotland's most
professional civil service departments, gave a weak smile
which could have meant anything. Then he beckoned
Gaunt to follow him out.

Gaunt nodded, touched Dan Cafflin on the shoulder
and indicated he'd be back, then followed Falconer out of
the hut. Falconer led the way across the waste ground outside then came to a halt near the edge of the canal bank. It
was a hot, sunny summer's day and the canal smelled of
rotted weed and worse.

"It's Saturday morning," said Falconer moodily, his eyes
on the dirty canal water. "I should be on a golf course.
Hell, even my wife knows Saturday mornings are for golf."
He scowled at his dark blue suit. "A man has to get rid of
his frustrations—that's elementary."

Gaunt waited, his hands in the pockets of the leather
jacket he wore over dark green slacks and an oatmeal-
coloured sports shirt. Across the canal, a family of ducks
were parading along the bank. He watched them, knowing
Falconer would get to what mattered.

"We've a little job needing done," said Falconer after a
moment. "You haven't too much on your plate right now."
He glanced towards the hut, where the car engine was still
throbbing. "How long will it take to put your new toy together again?"

"I'm due to collect it from Dan tomorrow." Gaunt eyed
Falconer carefully. As an external auditor in the department, he came under Falconer's control. And when Falconer went to work on a Saturday morning, that could
mean anything. "What's the job?"

"I want you to drive to Switzerland on Monday," said

Falconer. "To be more exact, the Remembrancer says you'll go."

"Drive?" Gaunt blinked at the notion. "Won't the budget rise to an airline ticket?"

"You're driving," said Falconer flatly. He was a desk man, and usually happy to leave it at that. But just occasionally he felt a twinge of envy for the external people, like now. He looked Gaunt up and down, sighing to himself, thinking of the department image. "The Remembrancer says you'll behave like a tourist on a holiday trip, in search of scenery, suntan, and ah—whatever the Swiss call sex." He considered Gaunt again and snorted. "That shouldn't be too difficult."

Jonathan Gaunt was tall, had a compact build, and was in his early thirties. If he owned anything approaching a business suit, Falconer had never seen it. He had a slightly freckled, raw-boned face, moody grey-green eyes, which gave a justified hint of occasional lapses in temperament, and untidy fair hair which even modern, relaxed civil service standards classified as too long.

He just didn't look as if he belonged. Falconer saw the grin beginning to play at the corners of Gaunt's mouth and felt a fresh irritation.

"Don't think it's going to be as good as it sounds," he said heavily. "Just get ready. You'll get your briefing and travel schedule first thing on Monday."

"But you know now." Gaunt knew Falconer liked being coaxed along. "Come on, Henry, what's it all about?"

"Something the Treasury people want us to handle," said Falconer. "A breach of the Exchange Control regulations, alleged currency smuggling."

"Big?" asked Gaunt.

"Probably—if it's genuine," said Falconer carefully. "We —ah—we're not even certain about that. But we could have a lead on a money-laundry operation, a group running a nice business taking out hot British pounds for customers and converting them into nice, cool, safe Swiss bank accounts."

"Every loyal British tax-dodger's birthright," murmured Gaunt.

"Exactly, and highly illegal." Falconer studied his wristwatch thoughtfully. "You know, there's a chance I could still play a few holes before lunch if I leave now."

"Switzerland, Henry," said Gaunt firmly. "Where, exactly? I might want to look at a map or something."

"The Montreux area, around there anyway," said Falconer. "It can wait till Monday. I—ah—yes, with luck I'll get some kind of a game."

He nodded to Gaunt and left, heading towards where he'd parked his car. A moment later it was driving away and vanished from sight down a lane.

Gaunt grimaced at the ducks, who had taken to the water and were paddling past. Then he turned and went back into the hut. Dan Cafflin was still absorbed with the throbbing engine and, leaving him to it, Gaunt wandered over to the car it had come from.

He had bought the British-built Chrysler Alpine a week before for the simple reason that his old black Mini-Cooper was worn out. The Chrysler was bigger but not too big. More important, it had been the showroom's demonstration car so he'd been able to get a substantial discount —and in Gaunt's current financial state that mattered. Particularly when the trade-in price for the Mini-Cooper had been even less than he expected.

Gaunt still reckoned he'd done well enough. He'd removed a few items from the Mini-Cooper, like the high-backed rally seat, which was now in the Alpine, the extra spotlamps, and the radio, which usually worked if you knew where to kick it.

The Chrysler was certainly a change, though it was front-wheel drive like the Mini had been. He'd brought it straight to Dan Cafflin from the showroom, and now the real problem remaining was the way it had hammered his bank account into the red.

The purr of the engine stopped. He turned and Cafflin beckoned an invitation towards a flask of coffee and two chipped cups. He joined Cafflin, they shared the coffee, and Gaunt broached another problem.

"Mind if I pay you at the end of the month, Dan?"

Lip-reading, Cafflin grinned and shook his head. Then he picked up a stub of pencil and scribbled on a grimy note-pad showing the result to Gaunt.

"Longer?" Gaunt thanked him with a grin. "No, I can manage it then."

He hoped so, anyway. Sipping his coffee, he turned his attention to the engine.

Dan Cafflin's method of tuning amounted to simple craftsman improvement of production-line products. Give him an engine and he stripped it down completely then began hand-polishing and refining each part until he was totally satisfied. He only changed a few items like valve springs then began a slow, careful rebuild.

But the result was always a revelation, a unit with amazingly increased power and efficiency to an almost unbelievable degree.

Cafflin gave him a nudge and began writing again. Relaxing back, Gaunt waited.

They'd first met three years earlier, in a military hospital. Lieutenant Gaunt, Parachute Regiment, had a broken back after a partial 'chute failure on a routine training drop. Sergeant Cafflin, Royal Tank Regiment, had been blown up by a land-mine in one of those small Arab Trucial State wars where there were always a few British military advisers around. Gaunt was discovering he'd more than a broken back to contend with and Cafflin was beginning the struggle to live without speech or hearing.

They'd been invalided out by the same medical board, lost touch for a spell, then met again by chance one day in Princes Street. Each with his own experience of adapting to civilian life and, by Gaunt's reckoning, Cafflin having made the better job of it.

The notebook was shoved under his nose again. He read the fresh scribble, grinned, and shook his head.

"No way," he said. "I know your idea of one quick drink. That damned car's got to be ready for Monday or I'm on the chopping block."

Cafflin threw back his head, opened his mouth, and gave the strange, whooping sound which meant he was laughing.

Then he got back to work.

Edinburgh still basked in sunshine when Monday came round. Along Princes Street the girls wore their lightest summer dresses in a way that brightened the heart of many a dark-suited, perspiring businessman. Even the grim mediaeval bulk of Edinburgh Castle had a cheerful glint about its granite buttresses and wide-mouthed cannon.

Accustomed more to rain and gusting wind, the city blossomed as the temperature kept rising. A Court of Session judge allowed learned counsel to remove their horsehair wigs in his courtroom and was whispered to be wearing open-toed sandals under his silk and ermine robes. A blonde in a bikini caused a three-car pile-up when she crossed Lothian Road carrying a shopping basket. At the Zoological Gardens, they began worrying about the penguins and polar bears and solemnly hosed down the elephants.

George Street, the heart of the city's business centre, was equally affected. The flags which marked consular and government offices hung limply from their poles, as if praying for a breeze. A shimmer of heat rose from the grey-slate rooftops and even traffic wardens handed out their parking tickets with minimal enthusiasm.

When Jonathan Gaunt arrived at the Exchequer Office it was 11 A.M. and the doorman had retired deep into the shade of the entrance hall. He walked up to the second floor, where the Remembrancer's Department was located, conscious of a general air of lethargy round.

Henry Falconer's secretary, a tall, well-built brunette in her early thirties, raised a significant eyebrow at his arrival then glanced at her watch.

"I'm late," agreed Gaunt.

"I've heard," she countered dryly.

He grinned and went through into Falconer's office.

"And exactly where the hell have you been?" asked Falconer indignantly as he entered. The Remembrancer's senior administrative assistant glared up from his desk as Gaunt let the door click shut behind him. "I wanted you here first thing this morning, remember?"

Gaunt nodded. Falconer had shed his jacket, which didn't happen often. Sweat beaded the older man's broad face but his tie was still stubbornly knotted and not a single button of his waistcoat was undone.

"You look hot, Henry," he said sympathetically. "Like you need a new thermostat fitted. Why don't you take Hannah out for a long, cool drink somewhere?"

"Because my wife would find out," growled Falconer. "All right, where have you been?" A sudden, worried thought crossed his mind. "Nothing wrong with your car, is there?"

Gaunt shook his head, brought over a chair, and sat down opposite him.

"I went to talk to a man," he soothed. "You said Exchange Control and you said Switzerland. He knows about them both—and Swiss banks. It was like taking a crash course on how the Mafia works."

"I could have told you that much on my own," grunted Falconer. "The average Swiss bank won't admit what day it is unless you've an account number." He frowned. "Who was he?"

"He was in banking, but retired," said Gaunt.

The little man was in a cell in Saughton Prison and would be for a spell to come. But he had been a banker, until he'd tried to get to Switzerland with a suitcase full of the bank's money. He'd been happy to talk about where he'd gone wrong and how it should be done, but somehow Gaunt felt Falconer wouldn't appreciate the situation.

"Well, advice always helps," said Falconer wearily. His eyes strayed to Gaunt's open-necked shirt. "For instance, I can remember a time when people in this department came to work properly dressed."

"Or they were charged with indecent exposure?" asked Gaunt. His grey-green eyes twinkled. "I'll bet even God upstairs left his woollie underwear off this morning."

Falconer winced at the irreverence to their departmental head but let it pass. He opened the thick file in front of him and flicked through the contents in silence for a moment.

Gaunt waited, listening to the steady, old-fashioned tick of the grandfather clock which Falconer kept in one corner of the office. The clock, its brass face glinting like a mirror in the sunlight, was there because Falconer's wife wouldn't give it houseroom.

He'd only met Falconer's wife once, and that had been enough. But it hadn't reduced the healthy respect he had for Falconer's shrewdness and contacts—and the Remembrancer's Department was a section where both were needed.

Always had been. The mediaeval Remembrancer had been a body servant to the early Scottish kings and queens, a cross between a walking notebook and an uneasy conscience. He'd had the role of remembering things for them —unless he knew they'd rather forget.

From that the present had evolved, a small but active civil service department which got involved in most things that mattered to Scotland—particularly the problems which larger, more hidebound departments couldn't take on. It worked with other people's cast-offs, from processing "state intelligence" to taking care of the Scottish crown jewels, from keeping an eye on the running of the law courts to keeping a record of every registered business company in the country.

And a whole lot more. The antiquated, centuries-old title concealed a department which kept a deliberately low profile until it had to show its real power.

"Yes, everything's here," said Falconer suddenly, looking up. He closed the folder, pushed it across to Gaunt's side of the desk, then used a handkerchief to mop some of the trickles of perspiration from his brow. "Hannah's done her usual packaging—full background briefing, routes, timings, all you'll need." He shook his head. "You know, I'd like that woman to make a real mistake once—just once."

"As long as your wife didn't find out?" suggested Gaunt.

"She would," said Falconer. "You still don't know much about women, do you?" He stopped there and flushed. "I'm sorry. That was a damned stupid thing to say."

"Forget it," said Gaunt, though it had been like scraping an old wound and they both knew it. "Just keep your secret lusts to yourself."

"I do." Falconer gave an embarrassed smile. "Ah—let's start with the basics, then. The Exchange Control regulations amount to control and restriction on the movement of private U.K.-owned capital either coming in or going out of the country. It takes a genius to understand even half of the fine print, but thank God we don't have to go that far."

"Amen," agreed Gaunt.

Currency dealing was legitimate if you were an operator in the money market, an oil sheik, or a bank. But if you were John Smith, private citizen, the ground rules were very different. The background was understandable and to a large degree international. If there wasn't some kind of control there would be constant stampedes across the currency markets. Even children would be out trying to swap their pocket money for German marks one week or French francs the next.

"If my kind of money is suddenly worth more than your kind of money—" Falconer paused and shrugged. "Well, there's a profit in it for someone and a loss for someone else."

Gaunt saw there was a lecture coming and that there was nothing he could do about it. He found his cigarettes and lit one, then settled back.

"Plenty of people in the U.K. have money they'd like to get into a happier currency than sterling," said Falconer. "Every time the pound takes a battering they bleed. On top of that, some of their money is 'hot' in terms of the taxman not knowing it exists." He thumbed towards the folder. "So they're ready customers for the money-laundry game—a guarantee to smuggle their money out to a nice, safe Swiss bank and have the cash converted into Swiss francs."

"Fixed-price contract," mused Gaunt, remembering his prison-cell session. "And it doesn't come cheaply."

"But a lot less expensive than paying tax," said Falconer. "Damned efficient too. A Customs squad nailed the last big money-laundry operation we had a lead on—they were smuggling sack-loads of money across the North Sea by weekend yachtsmen, and offering what amounted to all-risks insurance cover."

Gaunt grinned. It was the wrong thing to do.

"What's so funny?" demanded Falconer, and stabbed a stubby forefinger at him. "Try laughing this off. You like to play the stock market, right?"

"Pocket-money style," Gaunt reminded him. Falconer was one of the few people who knew that particular weakness, which kept on only because a stockbroker named John Milton, whimsical enough to have the telegraphic address Paradise Lost, had a sense of humour. "I'm the original small-time gambler."

"Who'd be better at bingo," agreed Falconer. "But if you wanted to buy stock in most foreign companies you'd have to pay a dollar premium which Her Majesty's Government would pocket. The smart boys don't. They use cash lying outside Britain, and laugh at your kind of ordinary idiot."

"And this time?" queried Gaunt, deciding he had to edge Falconer back to what mattered before the lecture became a sermon.

"Four days ago the Treasury office received a letter—anonymous, inevitably—posted in Geneva. They took one look, saw it said Scotland, and passed it on to us." Falconer lifted a single photostat sheet from the other papers on his desk and pushed it across. "Here's a copy. I like the—ah—economy in wordage."

Reading the photostat, Gaunt whistled softly. Economy was right, but the impact remained.

A CURRENCY SMUGGLING WILL TAKE PLACE FROM SCOTLAND TO MONTREUX NEXT MONDAY, USING SAFARI

SUISSE. THIS IS BECAUSE OF RECENT DIFFICULTIES IN
OTHER ARRANGEMENTS YOU MAY KNOW ABOUT. THE
STERLING INVOLVED IS IN EXCESS OF TWO MILLION SWISS
FRANCS.

He looked at it again. The handwriting was bold and
positive, the figure seven in the date had been crossed,
Continental style.

"A lot of laundry," he admitted.

"Dirty laundry," said Falconer. "All the handwriting experts can say is it could have been written by a woman—
something about the shape of the loops. Ever heard of Safari Suisse?"

Gaunt shook his head.

"Well, if this is a genuine tip-off—and God knows why
we should get it—then the shipment goes out this evening,
courtesy of the Royal Automobile Club, whose patron happens to be the Queen." Falconer swallowed and added
hastily, "That's incidental, of course."

"I'm glad," said Gaunt with sarcasm. "Tell me the rest."

"Auto-tourist safari is a package-deal way to drive across
Europe." Falconer prowled out of his patch of shade and
strode restlessly around the office. "You use your own car,
they make all bookings, schedule your daily mileage and
overnight stops, everything. There's a British Rail car-
sleeper train leaving Waverley Station this evening. The
bookings include a Safari Suisse of five cars, heading for
Montreux. Or it was five—it's six now, counting you."

"And they'll stick together, like a wagon train." Frowning, Gaunt rubbed his chin. "What do I do? Ride shotgun?"

For a moment Falconer's eyes hooded strangely, then he nodded.

"In a way. You'll try to decide the one we're after, the car carrying the money. These safaris don't rush things. You drive onto a cross-channel ferry at Dover tomorrow morning, and after that there's three days driving before you reach Montreux. You'll have time to sort them out."

Gaunt blinked. "Why do it the hard way? Half a million pounds is a lot of paper, even if it's in large denomination notes. The Customs squad at Dover could take these cars apart and—"

"No." Falconer stopped him. "We want the real operators, not their errand boys. That means following right through. There's no other way."

"If the tip-off is for real." Gaunt had been watching Falconer closely and something about the senior administrative assistant's manner was beginning to sound a warning. "All right, Henry, what's the little surprise you've been saving?"

Falconer hesitated, then gave a slightly sheepish nod.

"I—ah—was coming to that. His name was Edward Woods, a watch salesman from Liverpool."

"Was?" Gaunt raised an eyebrow.

"Was," admitted Falconer. "He was driving to Montreux five weeks ago. The Swiss found what was left of his car, burned out at the bottom of a mountain pass."

"How about what was left of Woods?"

"The same. It all appeared to be just another road accident."

"But?" persisted Gaunt.

"It was his fourth trip to Montreux this year. Nobody

saw the accident." Falconer permitted himself a slight shrug. "The wreck was examined of course, what was left of it, but the Swiss found nothing—except some unusual alterations to the bodywork, enough to hide away most things that might interest a smuggler. If Woods was in the currency game then either he'd already delivered or it had been—ah—"

"Removed?" Gaunt swore to himself. "Stop being polite, Henry. Hi-jacked?"

"Our tip-off says 'difficulties in other arrangements.' Anything's possible. Just remember, there's no law in Switzerland against bringing in foreign currency, smuggled or otherwise. They're more likely to give out medals."

Gaunt nodded. "Suppose I'm lucky and everything clicks?"

"You follow through, right to the delivery—then report back, nothing else," said Falconer. "After that—well, even the Swiss owe us some diplomatic favours as far as their end is concerned. Then we can backtrack to the British end of the organisation, and their customers. The Exchange Control Act has plenty of teeth, sharp enough to deal with anyone."

The internal 'phone on his desk buzzed softly. Falconer pounced on it, answered, and murmured a quick agreement. Then he hung up, reached for his jacket, and began pulling it on.

"The Remembrancer wants me," he said.

"Lucky you," said Gaunt. Rising, he picked up the Montreux folder. "Well, I'll be on that train—and if you're good, I'll bring you back a cow-bell."

Nodding absently, Falconer fastened his jacket and

began shuffling some of the papers on his desk. Leaving the office, Gaunt let the door shut behind him then ambled past Hannah's desk.

She had her handbag open and was busy applying fresh lipstick. Her typewriter was empty and her desk was cleared. She flushed when he raised a mildly quizzical eyebrow. Saying nothing, Gaunt nodded cheerfully and kept on going.

He had a feeling Henry Falconer's appointment wasn't with the Remembrancer. But that was none of his business.

It was 10 P.M. when Jonathan Gaunt drove into Waverley Station. The heat of the day had given way to dusk and a light, cool breeze was playing along Princes Street. Up above, the floodlights were beginning their nightly magic, transformng Edinburgh Castle into a fairy-tale fortress.

A corner of his mind reacted affectionately to the sight. The rest of his attention strayed between the Chrysler, which was running as smooth as any sewing machine, and the first stage of what he had to do.

He turned down into Waverley Station, following the Dover car-sleeper signs. The rest of the station was quiet but he found a queue of cars already parked at the start of the car-sleeper platform and the train starting to load.

Adding the Chrysler to the queue, Gaunt collected his overnight bag, got out, and handed his keys to a waiting railwayman. Then he checked in at the reception kiosk and walked down the length of the train to locate his sleeper compartment.

It was in the second coach at the front. Gaunt put the

bag in his compartment, left the coach again as a big green diesel locomotive came into link up for the overnight haul, and set off back along the platform.

There were seven coaches at the front of the train, one a day coach, another a bar-buffet unit, and the rest sleeping-berth coaches. The only customers in the bar unit were a pair of smartly dressed, elderly women placidly sipping what looked like gin and tonics, and they looked out as he passed, giving him slight, friendly smiles.

After the coaches came a string of open flat-trucks, bridged by ramps and with the first of their cargo of cars already aboard. Another came bouncing along from the platform loading bay at that moment, stopped in place, and was properly anchored down with chains by a pair of railway loaders.

He walked past slowly, giving each car a glance. Thirty-four vehicles were scheduled for the journey, all booked to go on across the Channel from Dover. The early arrivals had brand-new G.B. plates at their tails, most were laden with holiday luggage, and nearly every windscreen boasted a scatter of labels.

But only a green Fiat station wagon showed a Safari Suisse label like the one he'd stuck to the Chrysler. Gaunt remembered the two women in the bar coach and smiled. According to the list in the Montreux file, which was now in his overnight bag, the Fiat's passengers should be Mrs. Elsie MacLean and Miss Norah Stewart, retired school-teachers, both in their sixties and from the golfing town of St. Andrews.

They didn't seem likely candidates. He kept on, then stopped short as his Chrysler came swaying along the line of trucks, braked in a way that made him wince, and was secured like the others.

He watched the job being finished, humming quietly under his breath. Dan Cafflin had done a good job, the way he'd expected. Now he was looking forward to the chance of giving the car its head on a stretch of French motorway. Expenses paid.

But the Chrysler still was a reminder of the way its price had knocked his bank balance sick. He could think of only one way out of that, and it was risky, a gamble.

These had been the mildest adjectives John Milton had used when that long-suffering stockbroker had seen him that afternoon, then listened and protested.

"Who in his right mind buys shares in a company going burst?" had been Milton's reaction.

Gaunt couldn't blame him. Rhuvalla Construction was a large engineering firm in so much trouble that its creditors were moving in—while its shares were being unloaded like trading stamps. Except that one or two optimists were in the market and quietly buying, apparently hoping for a last-minute reprieve.

And if they were right, Rhuvalla shares would take off again.

He shrugged, pushed the problem aside, and walked on. Then he quickened his pace as he saw another car with a Safari Suisse label had just arrived.

Two men wearing sports shirts and slacks, both in their thirties, climbed out of a blue Saab hatchback. Each had the inevitable overnight bag, one tossed his keys to the nearest railwayman, then both entered the kiosk to book in.

Gaunt followed them and made a show of studying a railways map while they talked with the reception clerk. The file listed them as Thomas Hubbard and Eric Dawson, both employed by an advertising agency in Aberdeen.

In the flesh, Hubbard was a balding, moon-faced man with an English accent. Dawson branded himself a Scot from the moment he opened his mouth and was thin and sallow with long mousey hair. As soon as they'd finished with the clerk they left again, headed across the station concourse, and went into the snack bar.

He let them go but kept an eye on the Saab until it was driven aboard the train. It was early on, but Hubbard and Dawson had to rate high on his probability scale.

The minutes ticked past, another half-dozen cars came to join the queue for loading, then at last another Safari Suisse vehicle coasted in.

It was a small, open Triumph sports car, powder pink and eye-catching. The girl aboard it took him totally by surprise. He stared in disbelief as she got out and a moment later the same disbelief showed on her face, then she came straight over.

"Jonny!" She looked at him carefully and shook her head. "No, I don't believe it."

"Hello, Anna." He grinned down at her. She was slim and small, and all the rest was like yesterday from her long dark hair to that snub nose and those sparkling hazel eyes. She wore white cotton slacks and a sleeveless suntop which was the same powder pink as her car. "All right, complete it. Tell me you're for Switzerland."

"Montreux." Then her eyes widened. "Now—no, don't tell me! You too?"

"Safari Suisse, both of us." But he was puzzled. "I saw the booking list. If there had been an Anna Dunn—"

"No." Her expression changed. "Mrs. Anna Hart now, Jonny. You didn't know?"

He shook his head. "But—"

"Married and widowed." She said it in a brittle, factual way. "He died six months back—we hadn't been married a year."

"I'm sorry."

"It happens." She took her overnight case from a hovering porter, waited till the man had gone, then considered Gaunt again. "You look fit, Jonny, I'm glad. I—well, I heard about you. All of it—the accident, then Patty."

"Like you said, it happens." Gaunt eyed her hopefully. "How about letting an old friend buy you a drink in the bar coach nearer train time?"

"I'd like that," she agreed quietly, then left him and went into the reception kiosk.

Hands in his pockets, Gaunt stayed where he was and continued to watch the steady trickle of arrivals. But at the same time memories were flooding back and he had to force himself back to the present as another of the cars on his list pulled in.

It was a rusting yellow Ford station wagon and a couple in their late twenties tumbled out, the man tall, slight, and fair, the woman a raw-boned redhead. They were laughing as the man helped a small boy from the rear seat and collected a case. The file said Frank Corran ran a small TV repair business in Glasgow with his wife, Maggie. Their son, Peter, was four years of age.

The Corrans had just entered the reception kiosk when

the last of the Safari Suisse cars arrived. It was another Ford, a green almost-new coupe, and the middle-aged couple aboard were named as James and Mary Walker from a village a few miles out of Edinburgh. He sold insurance, she worked part-time in a law office.

Mary Walker was driving. A plump brunette with a sour face, she waited behind the wheel until her husband came round to open the door for her. He was a sad, small man who walked with a limp and his wife let him trail behind as she went purposefully towards the reception kiosk.

Gaunt still put off going aboard the train until about five minutes before departure time. Then he went straight to the bar coach, which was beginning to fill up. The two elderly women were at the same table as before, a map spread in front of them, but none of the other customers were from the Safari Suisse group.

British Rail bar service was basic. Gaunt went to the counter, ordered a whisky, and was handed a sealed miniature bottle and a plastic glass with two ice cubes. Then he saw Anna Hart coming in at the other end of the coach, waved her over, and noted the barman's decided interest in her as she ordered whisky and lemonade.

That meant another miniature, another plastic glass with two ice cubes, and a small ring-top can. Gaunt paid, gathered up the load, and they managed to snatch a vacant table for two just ahead of a bearded man in a kilt and a tweedy woman who looked like his mother.

Once they'd settled and had poured their drinks, Gaunt raised his glass.

"Four years," he said. "It's good to see you again."

She nodded, and nursed her drink between her hands.

Gaunt had a picture of that evening four years back, the last time they'd met. They'd had a few months of being together, had enjoyed it without things becoming serious, and the Army had just posted him south.

Where he'd met Patty, who had been young and blonde and had married a uniform and a pair of parachute wings. Except it hadn't worked out, even before his accident. Patty had waited until he came out of hospital, then told him, and they'd agreed it was over. She'd remarried a year later. His name was Eric Garfield, he ran an electronics company, and Gaunt liked him. He was good for Patty, much older, able to cope with her in a way Gaunt hadn't managed.

"I kept hearing about you now and again," said Anna suddenly. "How is she?"

"Happy."

"Does it hurt?" she asked.

He shrugged. "I got used to it."

"You do." She glanced down, and for the first time he noticed the wedding ring she still wore. "Andy was in the oil game, doing well. Then there was an explosion on a drilling rig, a damned stupid accident—he was killed outright."

The train gave a jerk, then began to pull away from the platform, gradually gathering speed.

"Like my car?" she asked suddenly.

"Uh-huh." Deliberately, he matched her change of mood. "What gave you the Safari Suisse idea?"

"I saw it advertised and liked it." She paused. "And you?"

"The same," he lied. "I had some holiday time due and didn't know what to do with it."

"That doesn't sound like the old Jonny Gaunt." She sipped her drink. "But you're some kind of civil servant now, aren't you?"

"Low-grade, low-paid," he agreed, while the train murmured into the blackness of a tunnel. "What about you?"

"I work for a property firm." She gave a chuckle. "Pay's good, I enjoy it most of the time. We're industrial development orientated, buying and selling sites. Right now there's a lot of money in that game."

The tunnel ended. They finished their drinks while the train swayed on through the deepening dusk, past the long rows of houses which marked the outskirts of Edinburgh. Deciding it was time for another round, Gaunt went back to the bar counter.

Hubbard and Dawson, the men from the Saab, were in front of him in the queue. They ordered two cans of lager each and left with them. The Corrans were at another table, without their child, but the two elderly women had gone.

He took the new drinks back to Anna. They sat and talked about old times and laughed together at old jokes while outside dusk blended into night. Soon the train was rumbling through a black, almost featureless landscape under a faint, cloud-filtered moonlight.

"Enough," said Anna Hart suddenly, glancing at her wristwatch. "The odds are I'll be sea-sick on that damned ferry tomorrow. I'm going to need my sleep."

Gaunt followed her out of the bar coach and along the

swaying corridor. She stopped outside her sleeper compartment and opened the door, giving a glimpse of her bunk already made down for the night.

"I'm three along from here," said Gaunt.

"I know." Her eyes twinkled. "I asked the sleeper attendant. Jonny—"

"What?"

"Good night."

He nodded and kissed her lightly on the lips. She smiled, then stepped into her compartment and the door closed firmly.

Gaunt went to his own compartment, opened his overnight bag, laid the Montreux file on the bed sheets, then brought out the little bottle of painkiller tablets. They'd been part of his travelling kit ever since he'd left the hospital.

He hesitated, then took two of the small white pills and swallowed them. Train sleeper berths weren't made for his kind of back and, like Anna, he wanted to be sure of his rest.

The compartment was warm. He stripped the blankets from the bunk, then slipped naked between the sheets, picked up the Montreux file, and read it through again.

Falconer had been right. It was a thorough job considering the minimal time available. The Safari Suisse route, as described, didn't seem to hold problems. It set an easy-going tourist pace through to a hotel at Montreux overlooking Lake Geneva. Once there, he had two contact names in the town—both marked "Emergencies Only."

He turned to the next page, another photostat copy of the original tip-off letter, and studied it.

Two million Swiss francs, half a million in sterling, a million in U.S. dollars, give or take a few years pay at the edges to allow for exchange rate fluctuations. Even if the money laundry took a modest fifteen per cent this was no small-time operation.

And if the letter was right, the money was riding behind him on one of those flat-trucks. It was quite a thought.

The rest of the file gave the few details there had been time to gather on his fellow Safari travellers, including the dates when they'd made their travel bookings. The Walkers and the Corrans had both booked in early spring, but the others came much later—Hubbard and Lawson entering their Saab only a fortnight ago, Anna just before that, and the two retired teacher ladies being tail-enders who had made their reservations only a week ahead of leaving.

Ease Anna and the two elderly women from the immediate reckoning and it meant yet another reason for the two men being an obvious choice. Even if the obvious was what he had to guard against.

Gaunt got up, tore off the slip of paper with the contact names, tucked it inside his driving licence, then carefully and methodically ripped up the rest of the file till it was so much confetti. Then he threw the result out of the compartment window, a small handful at a time.

That done, he lay down again and turned off the bedlight. Lying in the darkness, listening to the rumble of the train, he grinned. Anna had heard he was "some kind of civil servant."

He'd drifted a year after he left the hospital. About all he'd had to offer the job market were a few university terms spent studying law and accountancy before the

Army. Then someone, somewhere had put that together with his service record and he'd joined the Remembrancer's team.

External auditor had sounded a grey, old-fashioned job, the kind he'd believed he needed. Instead, Jonathan Gaunt, aged thirty-four and a cast-off soldier, had suddenly found himself right back in the business of living again.

Like on this trip. Following the route of a man who had died.

He fell asleep a moment later, still listening to the rumble of the train.

It was morning and more than four hundred miles south when he awoke, with the train already drawn into a platform at Dover station. The carriage attendant who brought the ritual cup of tea and morning newspaper glanced at the tangle of sheets at the foot of the bunk and nodded sympathetically.

"A real roaster of a night," he sympathised. "But they say it's cooler over on the French side.

Once the door had closed, Gaunt gulped some of the tea and yawned himself awake on the edge of the bed.

He glanced at the crumpled sheets. It hadn't been the heat. He'd had the nightmare again, falling endlessly through space with a useless 'chute streaming above him. All the way down, with a scream shaping at the back of his throat and awaking just before the final impact.

It always came when he was starting out on something new. Sometimes it stayed, too. But that was another thing he'd learned to live with.

He swallowed more of the British Rail tea, picked up the newspaper, and turned to the financial section.

Like he'd expected, there was a story about Rhuvalla Construction's problems. The shares had fallen further, but there were still buyers. Rhuvalla's makeup, in plant and equipment terms, were cursorily dealt with.

Then he stopped and rubbed a hand across his unshaven chin, remembering something else about Rhuvalla and something Anna had said the night before.

Rhuvalla had been planning to expand. They'd bought over several derelict factory sites at key locations.

And Anna had said there was big money in industrial sites.

He grinned. He was going to have to make time for a telephone call before that car ferry sailed for France. He might be chasing half a million pounds across Europe, but if a long-shot gamble on a hunch brought him in even a couple of hundred pounds in a single deal that had its own priority.

It would make a certain bank manager feel happier about the way he'd bought the Chrysler.

CHAPTER 2

Shaved and dressed, Jonathan Gaunt stepped off the train
about fifteen minutes later into a bright and still cool summer morning. One by one the cars on the flat trucks were
being unloaded by a team of British Rail drivers then left
in neat, waiting ranks on the station parking lot.

Making his way through the bustle, he saw his Chrysler
had already left the trucks. It was over at the far end of the
parking lot, where the Safari Suisse cars had been given a
corner to themselves. He waited till a line of luggage trol-
leys rumbled past from another train then crossed to the
Chrysler. Unlocking the door, he had just tossed his overnight bag inside when a stocky, middle-aged man in railway
overalls appeared at his elbow.

"Mr. Gaunt?" The man eyed him quizzically.

Gaunt nodded.

"Mind—uh—proving it?"

He produced his passport. The man glanced inside,
handed it back, and grinned.

"I'm Harry Willis, from Customs," he told Gaunt.
"There's a news stand down the platform and a porters'
room just behind it. See you there?"

The man ambled off. Gaunt spent a moment or two
making a show of walking round the Chrysler, kicking the
tyres and making the kind of inspection any driver might

be expected to do, then followed. He bought a pack of cigarettes at the news stand, saw the open door just behind it,
and went in. Willis was there, slouched back in an old
chair, and the Customs officer greeted him with a cheerful,
professional calm.

"I don't know what's going on and I don't even think I
want to find out," he said, while Gaunt perched himself on
the edge of a table in the dull, dusty little room. "My boss
sent me here with a couple more of our lads to do a quick
rummage job. Check the Safari Suisse cars on that train
then report to you." He brought an odd-shaped bunch of
keys from one pocket, tossed them idly in his hand and
nodded. "It's done."

"And?" asked Gaunt.

"Depends what you're after," said Willis cautiously.
"You know that Triumph sports car—the one listed as
belonging to a Mrs. Hart?"

"Yes." Gaunt tried not to show his surprise. "What
about it?"

Willis shrugged. "She's got a gun hidden behind the
dashboard—a man-sized .38 Browning automatic, fully
loaded. I should report it, except I was told just tell you,
then forget."

"Thanks." Gaunt chewed his lip, thinking of Anna, trying to take it coldly and rationally. "What else?"

"Nothing." The Customs man's eyes twinkled. "Except
for that green Fiat the two old ladies are driving. They've
got it crammed with tea-bags and powdered milk, like they
were on an expedition." He paused and shoved the keys
back in his pocket. "Look, Mr. Gaunt, all we've done is a

quick turn-over job. But if a pro wants to hide a load of contraband in a car—" He stopped and shrugged.

"You've got problems," agreed Gaunt. "Still, you'd know what to expect, right?"

"Would I?" Willis gave a grunt. "To be sure, I'd need an industrial X-ray outfit and a cutting torch. We nailed a character last week who had the spare tyre packed with marijuana. Before that, I had one who had a double-skin petrol tank filled with watches." He smacked a hand against his chair. "Beginners—hell, your real pro does a cut and weld job, then hides the weld."

"So if one of the Safari Suisse cars is carrying anything, we're dealing with a professional," said Gaunt softly. "That's what we thought. But at least you've confirmed it."

"Right." The Customs man got to his feet and gave Gaunt a sympathetic grin. "They'll clear Customs in the usual way at the ferry terminal—it'll be a wave-through job. That's arranged. And—uh—don't worry about the railway staff here. They saw us, they know us, but they'll keep their mouths shut."

Willis left him. Alone in the dull little room, Gaunt swore softly under his breath at the one hard fact the Customs man had been able to give him. Anna and a gun—it just didn't add up, not when he remembered the way she had talked and the things she had said.

But it had been four years since they'd met. Four years was a long time and people changed. His mouth twisted at the thought of what four years had done to him. Even so, there could be more than one reason why that .38 was under the Triumph's dashboard and he could afford to wait.

Going out onto the sunlit platform, he paused to light a cigarette and looked around. Willis had vanished, the last of the cars was being unloaded from the flat-trucks, and a steady trickle of passengers were leaving the front section of the train and heading for the parking area to claim their vehicles. The first few were beginning to drive off.

Gaunt joined the stream, noticing the Corrans and their small son just ahead. Maggie Corran had the boy by the hand while her husband struggled along beside them trying to keep the lid of their overnight case shut.

The youngster swerved across his mother's front, pointing excitedly towards a train coming in at another platform. Maggie Corran almost fell over him, collided with her husband, and the case flew open. A collection of clothes and toys scattered across the platform while Corran swore despairingly.

Grinning, Gaunt helped Corran gather things up and shove them back in the suitcase. Behind them, Maggie Corran stood tight-lipped, watching, the four-year-old at her side suddenly very quiet and slightly apprehensive.

"Thanks," said Maggie Corran as Gaunt finished. She glanced at her husband. "I told him that case was no good, but as usual he didn't listen."

"It's the lock," said Corran. "I thought I'd got it fixed." Picking up the offending case and nursing it in both arms, he shrugged. "Well, it's only from here to the car. Like Maggie said, thanks."

"We're on the same team," said Gaunt, indicating the

Safari Suisse label on Corran's case. "If it happens again, let me know."

Corran laughed good-naturedly. "I'll remember. But it's more likely to be car trouble next time—we're the original Switzerland or burst outfit."

He left the Corrans when they reached the Safari Suisse line-up in the car park. They were the last to arrive and the others, including Anna, were standing around a blue-uniformed R.A.C. patrolette. She was a cool, efficient blonde who counted heads, checked travel documents, then gave them a general, white-toothed smile.

"You've got your route-maps," she said brightly. "It's an easy, main road drive all the way and everyone always gets there—eventually." Pausing, expecting laughter, she didn't get it, forced a slight smile, and kept on. "You spend to-night at the Hotel Le Duc, at Villiers. That's less than two hundred and fifty kilometres from Boulogne so you've plenty of time for sight-seeing. Tomorrow's drive is about three hundred and eighty kilometres, and the day after that you'll cross into Switzerland and be at Montreux by the af-ternoon."

"How about coming with us, then?" asked a male voice unexpectedly. A leering grin on his sallow face, Eric Daw-son nudged Hubbard who was with him beside their Saab. "We'd make room for her, right, Tom?"

It brought a chuckle or two from the rest of the group but the blonde ignored him.

"As you're travelling the same route you'll get to know each other," she said briskly. "But it'll help if I make the introductions now."

She read out their names. Last on the list were the two retired schoolteachers, the same grey-haired women Gaunt had seen in the bar coach. Mrs. MacLean was a tiny, bird-like woman and Miss Stewart could have been her twin except for an extra inch or so in height.

"Time to leave, I think." The patrolette glanced at her watch. "You'll get breakfast on the ferry. Enjoy your holiday everyone."

She left them and the group broke up, heading for their cars. The Walkers were first away in their green Ford coupe, the woman driving and wearing heavy sunglasses on her plump, ill-tempered face, her husband still fumbling to fasten his seat-belt as the car moved off.

Gaunt turned towards the Chrysler, saw Anna coming over, and waited with his hand resting on the door-handle.

"Not talking to people this morning, Jonny?" she asked.

"It's not my best time," he said mildly noticing the way she'd pulled her long, dark hair back in a pony-tail, tied with a pink ribbon to match her outfit and the Triumph's paintwork. "How did you sleep?"

"Like a log." She stepped closer as the blue Saab drove past them and frowned after it. "These two—Hubbard and Dawson, or whatever they're called—don't rate among my favourite people."

"Did they make you an offer too?" asked Gaunt.

"I just don't like them." She wrinkled her nose, then smiled past him at the Corrans, who were loading their four-year-old aboard their rusting station wagon. "The others seem reasonable, what I've seen of them."

Gaunt nodded, watching her, thinking of the gun hidden in the Triumph.

"Something wrong?" she asked with a slight frown.

"No." He gave her a deliberate grin. "Let's move."

They were the last two cars of the Safari Suisse group to clear the station area and from there to the harbour ferry marshalling yard was only two or three minutes of well-signposted travel. The big Sealink ferry was in and loading and police were directing the new arrivals into marked lanes for the Customs and Immigration queues.

Anna Hart's powder-pink Triumph was waved into a centre lane. Following, Gaunt was diverted left and lost sight of her car. He stopped the Chrysler behind a big car-camper outfit, switched off, and saw a vehicle about a dozen cars ahead of them had a cluster of Customs men around it with the driver out and arguing.

There was a public telephone box a few yards away. Getting out of the Chrysler, he went over to the box, then kept one eye on the line of vehicles while he lifted the receiver and began dialling. John Milton was the kind of Edinburgh stockbroker who usually got to his office on time in the belief that the early worm avoided getting the bird, and Gaunt now had two reasons for wanting to speak to him.

He fed change into the money slot as his call was answered, and a moment later Milton was on the line.

"Shouldn't you be in France or somewhere?" asked Milton acidly.

"That's next," said Gaunt. "They're winding up the elastic to drive the boat." He paused. Milton was about his own age, not too dissimilar in temperament, and they were reasonably friendly. But he wasn't sure how the stockbroker was likely to react. "John, will you go along with me on a couple of favours?"

"Like what?" Milton's voice held a sudden caution.

"The first one's easy. Buy me up to two thousand Rhuvalla ordinaries if they're still falling, then unload them without further instruction when they upswing. Wait till they double."

"That could mean waiting till we're both drawing a pension," protested Milton. "I told you yesterday. You can't make money backing hunches. Hell, it—it's immoral." He sighed over the line. "Anyway, what are you using for money?"

"My next pay cheque." Gaunt's eye rested on one of the innumerable pieces of graffiti scribbled around the walls of the booth. The suggestion it made was physically impossible, even for a circus acrobat. But it brought a grin to his face. "All right?"

"It's your pay cheque," agreed Milton dolefully. "What else?"

"Something different." Gaunt hoped his luck would hold. "How are your contacts in the property game?"

"Reasonable." Milton was puzzled.

"There's a girl called Anna Hart who says she works for an Edinburgh outfit, on the industrial side. She also says she's a widow and she's driving a Triumph sports car—"

"What the hell?" said Milton indignantly. "Look, Jonny, sort out your own women."

"I could. But I don't want to do this the official way," said Gaunt seriously. "She—well, it's a long story. But I want to know if she's real. I owe her that much."

There was a long pause on the line, then Milton sighed.

"All right. It's 'Be Kind to Idiots Week.' How do I let you know?"

"Hotel Le Duc, at Villiers," said Gaunt. Outside the box the line of vehicles had begun moving again. Cars waiting behind his empty Chrysler were revving their engines. "Leave a message for tonight."

"That's France, for God's sake," said Milton despairingly.

"I'd heard," agreed Gaunt, and hung up.

He reached the Chrysler with the line ahead of him almost empty and two of the drivers behind him starting to blip their engines impatiently.

Customs and Immigration clearance was a brief formality before the barrier pole lifted to let his car through. On the other side, there was a short strip of quay, then the ferry's lowered stern ramp waited. From there, crewmen signalled him on deeper and deeper into the long, dimly lit car deck until he stopped, tightly parked in the middle of a group of holiday cars with a string of heavy T.I.R. trucks all around them.

The atmosphere stank of diesel oil and exhaust fumes. He was glad to get out of it, leaving the car and climbing a companionway stair which brought him out on a passenger deck near the ship's cafeteria.

They were serving breakfast and he joined the queue. With orange juice, coffee, and soggy toast on his tray, Gaunt was turning away from the cash desk when he saw Hubbard and Dawson at a table just ahead. Nodding a greeting, not waiting for an invitation, he joined them.

"Busy ship," he said easily, sitting down and unloading his tray. "Ever done this Safari Suisse thing before?"

Dawson shook his head, his mouth filled by a chunk of

bacon sandwich. Hubbard, his round, pale face a blank mask, took a gulp of coffee and looked Gaunt up and down for a moment.

"First time," he said shortly. "You?"

"Same." Gaunt played the friendly tourist to the limit. "But I like the idea, I mean, suppose one of us had car trouble"

"Great." Hubbard gave a disinterested nod while his sallow-faced companion kept on chewing. "Same with accidents, right?"

"Exactly." Gaunt sipped his orange juice for a moment, then put down the glass. "What made you choose it?"

The men exchanged glances.

"We just picked it out of the book. The price was right," said Dawson, and shoved back his chair. "Tom, let's go and watch how they take this thing out of harbour."

They rose and left. Gaunt stayed where he was and finished breakfast in the cafeteria while the ship's engines began rumbling, whistles blew on deck, and a final siren blast announced they were under way. When he did leave and go out on deck, Dover was already far astern and the ferry was creaming her way through the open sea, pitching a little as she met an occasional swell, the usual escort of hovering gulls screaming above.

The Dover-Boulogne crossing took just under two hours and Gaunt spent most of it alone, leaning on the rail. But as the French coast firmed from a haze into solid coastline more passengers began to appear on deck. The Corrans went past, Frank Corran carrying Peter and pointing to the small fishing boats working near the shore.

"Mr. Gaunt, isn't it?" said a bright voice suddenly at his elbow.

He turned, to meet the small smiling faces of Mrs. MacLean and Miss Stewart. Their grey hair ruffled by the sea breeze, heavy cardigans buttoned to the neck, they were evidently enjoying themselves.

"We thought it was you," said Miss Stewart. "We've met everyone else, haven't we, Elsie?"

"Hunted them down," agreed Mrs. MacLean with a chuckle. "You're travelling alone, aren't you, Mr. Gaunt?"

"That's right." He steadied her arm as the ferry lurched in an unexpected swell. "It just happened that way."

"Mrs. Hart says you're old friends," said Miss Stewart innocently. "That's nice—for both of you." She gave a sound close to an embarrassed giggle. "What I mean is—"

"Norah is always tactful," said Mrs. MacLean, stopping her there. She beamed out towards the land, Boulogne now a positive outline ahead, and her small, bird-like face wrinkled with pleasure. "You know, I'm still finding all this hard to believe. Seeing it all again, I mean."

"You've been before?" asked Gaunt.

"Not to Switzerland. France, yes." She glanced at Miss Stewart. "But a long time ago, Mr. Gaunt—probably before you were born. Norah and I were over with the Red Cross, before Dunkirk."

"Then spent the rest of the war in a base-camp canteen near London," agreed Miss Stewart. "So—yes, it's exciting all right. Even the way it all happened, so—" Her voice faded suddenly and a surprising flicker of near alarm crossed her face. Then, weakly, she finished, "Well, so unexpectedly."

Mrs. MacLean flushed and frowned at her. The two women stood in uneasy silence for a moment while the ferry throbbed on. Then the ship's loudspeaker system began a first announcement that owners should start heading back towards the car deck.

"We've still the duty-free shop to visit," said Mrs. MacLean quickly. "You wanted a bottle of sherry, Norah, remember?"

Miss Stewart nodded an immediate agreement, they murmured a good-bye, and went off. Watching them go, Gaunt twisted a wry grin. If even the two retired schoolteachers had some little secret of their own, life was really going to get complicated. But he just couldn't bring himself to worry too much about them.

He went down to the car deck as the ferry began slowing for the approach into Boulogne harbour. On the way, he saw Anna Hart just ahead and caught up with her.

"Where have you been hiding?" he asked.

"In a corner," she said sadly. "I told you, I don't like boats or ships or whatever you call the damned things."

They went down a companionway stair and slowed at the bottom, moving with the queue of other drivers ahead.

"Share a table with me at dinner tonight?" asked Gaunt.

She brightened, nodded, and said, "I'll maybe feel like eating by then. Right now, all I want is to be miserable on my own."

The queue moved, they reached the car deck, and the last Gaunt saw of her was as she made her way aft in search of the powder-pink Triumph.

Unloading at Boulogne was a slow business. The port had a dockside union dispute in progress, which didn't help. Then the fact of having to work on such a sunny day seemed to have incited every French official to work at a perverse, Gallic, snail's pace.

One way and another, Gaunt's car was one of the last to clear the ferry terminal. It was over an hour before he drove the Chrysler out of the dockland and turned on the main N.1 route for the south and east.

But then, at least, he began to make good time. It was noon, the local traffic had thinned for lunch, and in less than ten minutes he overtook Hubbard and Dawson almost loitering along in their Saab. The Walkers in their green Ford coupe were next. As usual, Mrs. Walker was driving but spared time to give a nod of recognition as he hooted and passed.

Montreuil went by, then the Chrysler was cruising through green countryside where the occasional tractor churned a dust trail in the fields. The sleepy, deserted streets of some small village or the stark ranks of gravestones marking a World War One military cemetery became the main landmarks.

The Corrans were stopped and having a picnic near Abbeville and there were more and more military cemeteries once he had gone through the old town. Arras, Cambrai, and St. Quentin were roadside signposts—names written in blood in Europe's history.

He reckoned Amiens the halfway point in the day's route and stopped for a late sandwich lunch at a pavement café under the shadow of the city's old Gothic cathedral. Sipping a glass of wine, relaxing in the sun, he shrugged wryly to himself. If he was supposed to be a tourist, he might as well act like one while he could.

The road was busier when Gaunt started off again. Strings of massive truck-and-trailer units clogged traffic in both directions till he hit a stretch of the Lille-to-Paris autoroute. It was the chance he'd been waiting for, and for the next several kilometres he had the Chrysler at full bore, engine howling, Dan Cafflin's tuning wizardry sending the speedometer climbing until the needle was close to quivering off the clock.

Eventually, he had to turn off and the roads were narrow and busy again. But he was still grinning as he crossed a bridge over the river Aisne and saw Villiers, the overnight stop, just ahead.

Villiers had a travelling fairground camped on its village square. It was a noisy, busy splash of canvas booths, roundabouts, and stalls, and Gaunt had to drive round its edges, the wheezing fairground music drowning everything else before he reached the Hotel Le Duc.

It was an old, three-story building just beyond the square, with parking space in a courtyard through a stone arch at the rear. When he drew in, two of the Safari cars, Anna Hart's powder-pink Triumph and the Walkers' Ford, were already there.

Gaunt got out stiffly, his back playing up a little after the long drive. When he went into the hotel, carrying his overnight bag, the lobby had a stale smell of cooking and the woman at the reception desk was a fat blonde with badly chewed fingernails. There were no messages waiting for him and when he asked about Anna Hart the blonde shrugged her indifference.

"She went out, m'sieu," said the blonde. "She will be back for the evening meal. Everyone comes back by then."

Gaunt's room for the night was on the second floor. It was small, reasonably clean, and comfortable in an old-fashioned way and the window looked out across the square where the travelling fair was as noisy and busy as ever. He dumped his overnight bag on the bed, had a wash, and went down in search of the bar.

It was a cool, dark basement room where the only other customer was James Walker. Gaunt nodded to the slight, sad-faced insurance agent, ordered a whisky from the elderly bartender, then took his drink over to where Walker was sitting nursing a brandy.

"Good trip?" asked Gaunt, pulling out a chair and joining him.

"Ask my wife," said Walker with a faintly bitter smile. "She was doing the driving. I just called out the road numbers."

"I noticed," agreed Gaunt.

"That's how it is with us." Walker tapped his left leg. "I wrote off our last car when I hit a truck. Collected this limp, a six-month driving ban from a hard-line judge, and a fine to match." He swirled his brandy moodily. "For full details, ask my wife—hell, I didn't think she even knew some of the names she called me."

"And she doesn't let you forget?" suggested Gaunt, amused.

"That's an understatement," admitted Walker. "Can't blame her, I suppose. When you can't drive it plays havoc with my kind of job. Then she's carrying the full load on this trip, where we'd normally share it." He finished his drink, snapped his fingers at the bartender for another, then considered Gaunt again. "Been to Switzerland before?"

Gaunt nodded. "But not around Montreux."

"We've been a couple of times." Walker paused as his new drink arrived and the old glass vanished. "Scenery's good and it's in the French-speaking part. They're nice people—most of them, anyway. Maybe I prefer the German Swiss, to the north, even if their wine is like battery acid, but Mary says Montreux, so that's where we're going." He looked past Gaunt and winced slightly. "Here she comes. Escape if you can—the rules say I can't."

But the Mary Walker who bore down on them seemed in a relatively good mood. She ordered a champagne cocktail and settled in a chair, then her plump face beamed in Gaunt's direction.

"I've been at the fairground," she declared. "Look what I won at the coconut stall." She unwrapped the package on her lap, revealing the ugliest china dog Gaunt had ever seen. "Like it?"

"It's unusual," said Gaunt cautiously.

"Among other things," muttered Walker.

Mary Walker gave her husband a frosty, sideways glance, wrapped the package again, and took a quick gulp at her drink.

"They've more. I'll try for the pair tonight," she announced. Then as her husband winced, she added pointedly, "At least it makes a change from driving. Do you like fairgrounds, Mr. Gaunt?"

Gaunt made a neutral murmur and she went on. In the next few minutes he knew that she had her husband on a cholesterol-free diet, that she worked part-time to make up for the way Walker's income had dropped since his accident, and that by her reckoning she was the brains and ability in their marriage.

"Everyone needs a good anchor, Mr. Gaunt," she said. "That's what I try to give James—"

"You certainly do," said Walker. "None better."

The sarcasm seemed lost on her but Gaunt decided he'd had enough, made noises about having things to do, and left them to it. The fairground music took him out of the hotel, and as he went through the courtyard he noticed that Hubbard and Dawson's blue Saab was now parked and empty beside the other cars.

But Switzerland was still more than a day away. Lighting a cigarette, he went over to the fairground and wandered around it for a spell. It was the usual small touring outfit, complete with a few yawning, underfed animals in travelling cages and a row of living vans drawn up at the rear. The stalls and booths were packed with locals, their numbers swollen by a sprinkling of French soldiers obviously drifting in from an army camp.

Some things never changed. A reminiscent grin crossed his face at the way the army uniforms usually had a girl on one arm and a bottle of wine under the other. And from some of the scowls round, the local unattached male population didn't like it.

The rest of Villiers came down to a few shops, the church, and a tumble-down garage. He gave up, went back to the Hotel Le Duc as dusk began greying in, and saw all the Safari cars had arrived.

Anna Hart was back too. She had left a message with the fat blonde at the desk.

"Madame Hart says she will meet you in the bar before dinner," said the blonde, then leaned forward. "Perhaps, if m'sieu wishes a quiet table, you should book it now."

"Going to be busy?" asked Gaunt.

"*Oui.* Another Safari group is arriving—*Anglais* too, but

on their way home." She shrugged, her body quivering like
a massive jelly. "Most nights it is the same. People coming,
people going. They spend money on the way out, then
steal the ashtrays as souvenirs on the way home."

Gaunt took her advice about the table, then went up to
his room. He had about an hour to spare and spent most of
it sprawled on the bed, resting his back. Then, the gathering dusk outside now tinged by the bright glow of the fairground lights, he rose, put on a clean shirt, knotted a tie in
place, and went down.

The basement bar was busy with strangers, most of them
tourists, but he found an empty table and kept it that way
till Anna came in a few minutes later. She had changed
into a lightweight blue denim suit, the jacket belted at the
waist, and her hair, freed from its pony-tail again, had been
brushed until it gleamed under the dim lighting.

"So what happened to you?" asked Gaunt as she sat
down.

"The French Army," she said demurely. "They've an in-
fantry depot a few kilometres west of here. All I did was go
out to have a look round the fairground, and next thing a
couple of lieutenants are heaving me into a jeep and taking
me off on a guided tour."

"Congratulations," said Gaunt dryly. "On getting back,
I mean."

She laughed. "I coped with you, Johnny. Remember?"

He had no real answer to that one. They had a drink,
then went up to the Hotel Le Duc's shabby little dining
room. It was crammed, but the fat blonde had kept her
word and reserved them a corner table—and the food,
when it came, was superb. Duckling *pâté,* then a fish soup,

was followed by *boeuf* Bourguignon, and finally, in place of a sweet, they were presented with a cheese-board choice that could have been a meal in itself.

"What next?" asked Gaunt as they finished the last of their wine with a cigarette each. He looked around the crowded restaurant, exchanged smiles with Mrs. MacLean and Miss Stewart, who were a couple of tables away, then considered Anna thoughtfully. "If we try that fairground again—"

"No army," she promised with a mock solemnity. "I'll behave."

There was a noisy altercation going on when they walked through the hotel lobby on their way from the restaurant. Frank Corran was the cause but the night clerk now on duty, a sleek, worried-looking young man, was protesting almost as loudly.

"What's wrong?" asked Gaunt as they reached Corran.

"Ask him," said Corran angrily, his thin young face flushed. "Listen—you can hear it from here."

They listened and heard the muffled sound of a child howling.

"Peter?" asked Anna.

Corran nodded and glared at the night clerk again. "He was sleeping when we went down to eat. Now all we can get out of him is that a man came into our room. Maggie's trying to calm him down."

"But how could it happen, m'sieu?" protested the night clerk. He spread his hands in an appealing gesture to Gaunt. "*C'est impossible* . . . perhaps the child had a nightmare. There was no robbery, nothing was taken, no other guest complained. Perhaps—" He paused and brightened. "Did you leave your door locked?"

"No," admitted Corran. "Not with Peter there."

"Ah." The clerk nodded quickly. "Then another guest could have made a mistake, gone into the wrong room—"

"Maybe." Corran glanced at Gaunt. "But I don't like it. Would you?"

Gaunt shrugged. The wails from upstairs were fading. He had a feeling he'd like to check his own room but that would have been difficult without making it obvious.

"Well"—Corran scowled at the clerk again—"next time it happens, you'll hear a damned sight more about it."

The young TV repairman stumped off towards his room and the night clerk retired quickly and thankfully. But he gave Gaunt a nervous glance on the way, then followed it with a sickly smile.

"Do we try the fairground or wait here for the next entertainment?" asked Anna.

He grinned, took her arm, and they went out.

If the fairground had been busy earlier, nightfall had brought it to peak business. The strings of bright, coloured lights, fed by a thumping generator which couldn't be drowned by the fairground music, lit the crowded square while every booth had its full quota of customers. Stallholders bawled the attractions and prizes they had to offer, rifles snapped at the shooting gallery, and farming families rubbed shoulders with the inevitable soldiers and their girls.

They tried a couple of stalls, won a cheap ball-point pen for rolling coins at one, then drifted on through the cheer-

ful, jostling crowd. A glimpse of Mary Walker grimly in ac-
tion again at the coconut toss made them head in the opposite direction, past the pungent odour coming from the
animal cages, and they arrived beside a brightly lit, whirl-
ing merry-go-round.

A couple of well-wined young French *soldats* were cling-
ing to the same wooden horse, in danger of falling off as it
went swinging round. Anna was gripping his arm, laughing
at their antics, but Gaunt's attention was elsewhere.

Not far away, at the edge of the booths, Tom Hubbard
and Eric Dawson were talking to a tall, bearded stranger.
The stranger, smartly dressed and grim-faced, gave a curt
nod at something Dawson said. Then, after another brief
conversation between the three, the bearded man turned
on his heel and went away between the booths, out into
the darkness beyond them.

Gaunt switched his attention back to Hubbard and
Dawson. They talked together for a moment, Hubbard
grinning oddly, then headed off through the crowd in the
direction of the hotel.

The merry-go-round slowed, the two young *soldats* tumbled off, and Anna lost interest. In the next tent a busty
Nubian girl wearing a few spangles was starting a fire-eat-
ing act and they paid and went in.

It wasn't much of an act but the glint of the flames on
the Nubian girl's heavily oiled body made up for that as far
as the audience of locals and soldiers were concerned. They
clapped and cheered as she finished—then suddenly there
was a confusion of shouts and screams near the front and
the Nubian girl dived for safety through a rear flap in the
canvas.

A brawl had broken out between a group of soldiers and some of the locals. As bottles began flying and the fighting spread, the rest of the audience spilled back in a general stampede to get out. Swept along with the crowd, separated from Anna, Gaunt found himself in the open again. He caught a glimpse of her for a moment, on the edge of the crowd, then he lost sight of her as a squad of *gendarmes* and military police appeared from nowhere and charged into the tent to break up the fight, clubs swinging.

The rumpus died down, a few battered figures were dragged away, and Gaunt looked around again for Anna. He wasn't alone. Other people were searching for friends and family, but the slim, denim-clad figure he wanted had vanished.

The fairground had settled back to normal by the time he gave up and decided she'd gone back to the hotel. Starting off in the same direction, Gaunt reached the courtyard entrance, took a few steps across the cobbles, then stopped as he heard a strange, dragging noise, then a groan coming from beside the parked cars.

The groan came again, something moved in the shadows, and he hurried over. A man was lying doubled up on the ground beside a Renault with French registration plates. As Gaunt stooped, the man tried to move again, keeping one hand clutched tight against his side.

The man looked up. He was small, with long, black hair and sharp features and he was wearing a dark sweatshirt with matching slacks. With his mouth twisted with pain, he tried to speak, then suddenly his eyes widened, staring over Gaunt's shoulder.

Starting to turn, Gaunt heard a rustle of movement

behind him. Then something hard and heavy crashed against his skull and he only knew he was falling while pain exploded like a red flare inside his head.

He came round in a sick daze, vaguely hearing Anna's voice close beside him and aware that he had been dragged into a sitting position against the courtyard wall.

"Jonny, try and look at me," urged Anna again. "What happened?"

He forced his eyes open, saw her face as a blur with other blurs moving behind her, then managed to focus properly.

She was bending over him, had loosened his collar and tie, and her face was tight and worried. He forced a weak grin, looked past her, and saw the Walkers frowning down at him. Mary Walker was clutching another of the grotesque china dogs under her arm.

"Is he drunk?" asked Mary Walker stiffly.

"Don't be damned stupid," said Anna without glancing round. "Jonny—"

"Hold on." Wincing, his head throbbing, he let her help him to his feet, then leaned against the wall, looked around, and swore wearily.

The man on the cobbles had gone. So had the Renault.

"What happened?" insisted Anna.

"Somebody thumped me." He nursed his head with one hand, feeling a gathering lump but finding with surprise that the skin wasn't broken. Then he glanced at his watch. Only a few minutes had passed since he'd entered the courtyard. "You didn't see him leaving?"

"No." It was James Walker who answered, frowning

uneasily. "We were coming back from the fairground and met Mrs. Hart. She said she'd lost you somewhere. Then—"

"Then we found you," completed Anna. She looked at him closely. "There was no-one around, Jonny."

"Were you robbed?" asked Mary Walker with a frosty curiosity.

He felt for his wallet. It was reassuringly there, in his inside pocket. He hesitated, about to tell them about the man on the cobbles, then changed his mind.

"If it wasn't robbery, maybe you got in the way of some hassle left over from the fairground fight," suggested Walker. "That would make sense. The army and the locals will have a few brushes before tonight's out—I'll bet on it."

Gaunt nodded and told them, "Forget about it. I'm in one piece, so why make trouble?"

Walker and his wife exchanged a glance. Then, Walker in the lead for once, Mary Walker still clutching her ridiculous china dog, they went into the hotel. Still leaning against the wall, Gaunt made a slow business of lighting a cigarette, drew on it, then grimaced at Anna.

"What really did happen?" she asked quietly.

He shrugged with feeling and admitted, "I wish to hell I really knew."

Which amounted to the truth.

The lobby was deserted when they entered the hotel. Wearily, Gaunt climbed to the second floor, reached his room, and grinned wryly at Anna.

"This isn't what I had in mind," he told her. "But thanks—and good night."

She hesitated, then nodded seriously and left him.

Once she'd gone, Gaunt unlocked his door and went in.

Going over to the washbasin, he turned on the cold-water tap, stuck his head under it for a couple of minutes, and felt better.

Water still dripping from his hair, he made his way across to the window. The fairground was still in full swing down below in the square, nothing seemed to have changed.

Except there had been a wounded man in that courtyard —or a man who had acted that way. Then he had gone, or had been taken away.

Gaunt reached for his cigarettes again, brought them out, then for the first time saw a dark stain on his jacket sleeve. He looked at it more closely, and his mouth tightened. It was blood, still moist to the touch.

Which removed one doubt.

Going back to the washbasin, he washed away all trace of the stain, draped the jacket over a chair to dry, then saw something else as he turned away.

When he'd gone out, he'd left his overnight bag lying open on the bed and had tossed his discarded shirt on top of it. The shirt was still there, but the bag had been neatly closed.

Grimly, angry, he went back downstairs in his shirt-sleeves, through the empty lobby, and out into the courtyard. There was no sign of blood or any other trace where the man had been. But he'd more or less expected that too.

Drawing a deep breath, he walked across to Anna Hart's open sports car, got in, and ran his hands carefully under the tangle of wiring behind the dashboard. His fingers closed on a small, cloth-wrapped bundle, he brought it out, and in another moment the cold, black metal of the .38

Browning the Customs man had found lay in his hands. He sniffed the barrel, then, satisfied it hadn't been fired, wrapped the gun again and put it back in its hiding place.

The blue Saab was two along. But when he tried it, the doors were locked. Shrugging, he went back into the hotel. The night clerk was at the reception desk again.

"You," said Gaunt softly. "Come here."

"M'sieu?" The man came over reluctantly.

"*Aide-moi,*" said Gaunt. Then, suddenly, he grabbed the man's tie with one hand and yanked him face-to-face. "One question. Who got the pass-key?"

The clerk stared at him open-mouthed, then gave a strangled squeal as Gaunt twisted his grip and the tie tightened.

"Me, or the police," said Gaunt softly. "Take your pick. Who got the pass-key?"

"I—m'sieu, I swear I don't know," gasped the man, sheer fright in his eyes. "It was taken, yes—for half an hour, then it was back." He stopped, near to tears. "It hangs on a hook beside the desk. But that is all I know, m'sieu—truly."

Gaunt let him go, sensing he wasn't lying.

"Thanks," he said dryly, then tossed a twenty-franc note on the desk. "The two men with the Saab—Hubbard and Dawson. Are they in?"

The clerk nodded, rubbing his throat. "*Oui,* m'sieu. Maybe ten minutes ago, maybe more. They ordered a bottle of whisky and I took it up to their room." He moistened his lips. "If you desire anything—"

"A new head, that's all," said Gaunt viciously, and went up to his room.

Even with two of the painkiller tablets to help, he took a long time falling asleep.

Things were going wrong, happening in a way he hadn't anticipated. He knew he had to find out why, and soon—before they got worse.

CHAPTER 3

The fat blonde girl was back behind the hotel desk when Gaunt came down in the morning. From the cautiously interested way she greeted him it was plain the night clerk had given her some kind of version about what had happened.

But there was still no message for Gaunt. Disappointed at John Milton's apparent delay, he went over to the door and looked out at the sunlit courtyard. Most of the returning Safari's cars had already left for the Channel ports and others were getting ready to depart. The only early starters from his own group, however, appeared to be Mrs. MacLean and Miss Stewart. Their green Fiat station wagon was gone from the line-up, leaving a small pool of sump oil where it had been overnight.

He found breakfast being served in a glassed-in patio area and got a table to himself next to the Corran family. They were almost finished and Maggie Corran had just stopped their infant son from trying to upend the coffee pot.

"How do you feel now?" asked Frank Corran, nodding a greeting. He thumbed along the patio to where the Walkers were eating. "Mrs. W. has been telling everyone you were mugged last night."

"Or were drunk," said Maggie Corran with a malicious edge. "She hinted she wasn't sure."

"Her privilege." Gaunt wondered if Mrs. Walker would have swapped heads with him, complete with the tender, lumping bruise he now possessed. "All I did was stray into someone else's hassle. Have you had any more visitors upstairs?"

"No," said Maggie Corran thankfully. "But Peter's still talking about that man."

"Bad man," said the cheerful four-year-old on cue. "Not like him. Mummy says Daddy should have got the cops."

"God help us when he's older," sighed Corran. "Come on, you—"

He lifted his son from the chair, nodded to his wife, and they rose.

"See you along the way," said Corran, and his mouth twisted whimsically. "We had our honeymoon in Montreux six years ago." He glanced at his wife. "Never thought we'd be able to afford to see it again, did we?"

"Who says we can?" she asked pointedly.

"True." Corran paused, then shrugged. "Never mind, Maggie. Let's go and scare the hell out of a few more French drivers."

The Walkers were leaving too. James Walker gave Gaunt a sympathetic nod as they passed his table but Mary Walker studiously ignored him. Gaunt swore under his breath at the woman, then his coffee and rolls breakfast arrived and he concentrated on that.

A few minutes later, as he was lighting a cigarette to go with the last of the coffee, both cars pulled away from the courtyard and drove past the patio. He watched them turn right at the square, then as the cars vanished along the main road he sat back for a moment and drew on his cigarette.

Lump any group of strangers together and some odd aspects about them were bound to turn up. But this Safari Suisse group was as mixed as they came, and what had happened the night before held its own warning—that his mission for the Remembrancer was shaping in a more difficult and dangerous way than he'd ever anticipated.

As if to underline it, another car snarled out of the courtyard. It was Hubbard and Dawson in their Saab. Tight-lipped, almost certain they were the key, he watched the blue car turn right at the square as the others had done.

They were still a long way from Switzerland. Plenty could happen yet.

A little later Gaunt collected his overnight bag, checked out at the hotel reception desk, and left. He was in the courtyard, ready to get into his car, when Anna Hart came out of the hotel also ready to leave.

"Seems like we're the late brigade," she said without concern. Then, giving him a considered glance, she added, "You look a lot better than you did last night."

"I'm fit enough to murder that Walker woman," said Gaunt grimly.

"You heard?" Anna chuckled, turned away to throw her overnight bag into the Triumph, and faced him again. "Jonny, mind if I tail along behind you today? I'd never win a prize for map-reading."

"We can get lost together," he agreed. The idea suited him in more ways than one.

The two cars left the courtyard a few moments later, Gaunt in the lead as they joined the busy N.37 route. He kept the Chrysler at a steady pace, the powder-pink sports car always the same distance back in his rear-view mirror, and in less than half an hour they were skirting the town of Soissons, then were on a quieter road, signposted for Troyes, 150 kilometres to the south.

Gradually, the day got warmer and brighter. Gaunt wound down his window, reached for his sunglasses, and felt an occasional envy for the girl behind him in her open car while the road kept on through the gentle, almost empty French countryside.

The traffic stayed light for a long time. But suddenly, as he rounded a bend through a wooded section of road, Gaunt instinctively slowed at the sight of a line of vehicles stopped ahead. They included an ambulance and two police cars. Broken glass glinted on the tarmac, and a wrecked car was lying on its side in the ditch, men working around it.

In another moment he had a clearer view of the crashed car and his hands tightened on the steering wheel. It was a blue Saab and the men were gently lifting someone out of it onto a waiting stretcher.

Pulling in at the verge once he'd passed the other vehicles, Gaunt got out. Anna Hart stopped her car behind the Chrysler and joined him, her face pale and concerned.

"It's got British number plates," she said quietly.

He nodded silently and they walked back towards the crumpled Saab and a set of violent skid-marks on the road. As they got nearer, the smell of hot oil hung in the air.

Suddenly, Anna's hand gripped tight on Gaunt's arm. An elderly woman, her face a bloodied mask, her summer dress ripped and torn, was lying limp on the stretcher now being carried towards the ambulance. As the little knot of onlookers parted to let the stretcher through, Gaunt saw that the body of an elderly, heavily built man had been laid on the grass beside the wrecked car.

"Then it isn't"—Anna paused and moistened her lips—"when I saw the car, I thought it was Hubbard and Dawson."

"That makes both of us," agreed Gaunt. He looked beyond the car, to where a suitcase which had been thrown clear had burst open, scattering a litter of clothing along the edge of the ditch. "Poor devils, whoever they are."

A gendarme standing near overhead their voices and came over.

"If m'sieu is English perhaps he knew these people?" he asked hopefully.

Gaunt shook his head.

The gendarme shrugged his disappointment. A fat, middle-aged man with a small moustache, he tucked his thumbs in his pistol belt and considered the wreck.

"*Touristes* . . . it is the season for this kind of thing," he said dispassionately. "The man is dead, of course. The woman may live but she is badly hurt."

"Is there anything we can do?" asked Anna, watching the stretcher being loaded into the ambulance.

"*Non.*" The gendarme gave her a slight smile. "We have reasonable experience in such things, believe me. Except"—he scowled at the wrecked car—"except in maybe the way this happened."

Gaunt took out his cigarettes and offered the man one. The gendarme took it, accepted a light, and nodded his thanks.

"What did happen?" asked Gaunt.

"A *camion* . . . a truck." The gendarme's scowl deepened and he thumbed towards the other onlookers. "We have one witness who was driving behind them. This *camion* overtakes, cuts in—a big, heavy truck. Smash, and the car is off the road, like this. But the *camion* does not stop. What you would call a hit-and-run."

"Leaving them like that?" Anna stared, horrified, at the man.

He nodded, took another draw on the cigarette, nipped it, then carefully tucked the stub away in a tunic pocket.

"It happens, ma'mselle," he said. "But we will find it, and the driver."

Turning, he left them and headed back towards the crashed car. The ambulance was pulling away, emergency lights flashing and siren beginning to wail. A first few flies were buzzing around the dead man and someone had covered his face with a jacket from the scattered clothing.

Slowly, Gaunt and Anna began to walk back towards their cars. The verge, he noticed, was thick with wild poppies. He could hear cattle in the distance.

"Jonny," said Anna in a surprised voice.

He saw for himself. Eric Dawson was leaning against the side of her car, waiting on them. The familiar blue Saab was drawn up in front of Gaunt's car, with Hubbard lounging behind the wheel, looking back at them.

"How the hell did that happen?" asked Dawson as they reached him.

"A truck that kept on going," said Gaunt.

"Just like that?" Dawson's thin, sallow face showed something close to agitation. "Who says?"

"Somebody who saw it," said Gaunt flatly. "When we

saw the car, we thought it was yours. You were ahead of us."

"We stopped at Soissons." Dawson moistened his lips. "Luck of the draw, you could call it. Uh—who were they?"

"Tourists," said Anna. "Two of them. The woman might live."

"Makes you think. Might as well get moving, eh?"

He walked quickly to the Saab, got in, nodded to his companion, and it drove away.

"Makes you think," repeated Anna bitterly as the car vanished round a bend. "He didn't really give a damn, did he?"

"Maybe he's just glad it wasn't them," said Gaunt. "Ready?"

She sighed, got into the Triumph, and started it up. Gaunt climbed into his own car, started the engine, then looked round to make sure the road was clear before he pulled away. A black B.M.W. with Swiss registration plates was slowly passing the accident area, the driver craning to see what he could, and Gaunt waited.

The B.M.W. reached him, began to accelerate again, and Gaunt stiffened as he saw who was behind the wheel. It was the same tall, bearded man who had been with Hubbard and Dawson at the fairground. For a moment, as the black car passed, the stranger glanced in his direction and their eyes met.

Then the car had gone. Behind him, Gaunt heard Anna blip the Triumph's engine in a minor show of impatience. Lips pursed, he put the Chrysler into gear and set it moving. A glance in the rear-view mirror showed the Triumph following.

Things were crowding in on him. Driving on, the kilometre markers slipping past while the road wound through the same, apparently endless farming landscape, Gaunt tried to marshal his thoughts again.

That another blue Saab from Britain had been travelling on the French road at the time Hubbard and Dawson's car should have been there was sheer coincidence. That it had been forced off the road and wrecked by an apparent hit-and-run truck might be dismissed as brutal bad luck. But add the rest and the bearded man now driving somewhere ahead, and Gaunt's already overstrained credulity collapsed.

Someone else knew that a fortune in smuggled currency was travelling with the little Safari Suisse convoy. Knew it, and was ready to carry out cold-blooded murder in the process of hi-jacking the consignment, no matter how many innocents were caught in the middle.

Angrily, he kept his foot down on the accelerator and took the Chrysler hard and fast round a sudden bend in the road in a way that made the tyres scream and brought a blare of indignant air-horns from a truck-and-trailer outfit coming in the opposite direction. That brought him back to reality and, cursing at his own stupidity, he eased back and allowed Anna to catch up again.

His own role, he knew bitterly, remained the same. Watch and wait, whatever happened. The Remembrancer's Department had its own, over-riding priorities.

Another hour of steady travel brought the time to midday, when the old cathedral town of Troyes appeared ahead. By then the weather had started to change, heavy grey clouds beginning to build up in the previously blue

sky. When they stopped at a filling station to top up the
cars' tanks, Anna took the chance to clip the Triumph's
canvas hood into place.

They also decided it was time to eat, and a few minutes
later they stopped again, near the centre of town where a
small restaurant looked out toward the slow, lazy water of
the river Seine.

The meal was good, the *patron*, a fat, fussy little French-
man, served them personally, and Gaunt welcomed the
break and the chance it gave him to stretch his back muscles. But Anna stayed quiet, even though he caught her
eyeing him several times in a strangely thoughtful way.

At last, just as he'd paid the bill and was ready to leave,
she laid a hand on his arm and stopped him from getting
up.

"Jonny, can I ask you something even if it sounds crazy?"
she said in a low, earnest voice.

"Go ahead," he invited mildly.

She took a deep breath. "Is this really just a holiday trip
as far as you're concerned?"

Taken by surprise, he still managed a grin. "That depends what you've got in mind. Maybe I'll do a deal with
some Swiss banker, agree to marry his daughter who happens to be as ugly as sin—" He stopped, seeing no amusement on her face, and became serious. "What's worrying
you, Anna?"

"Nothing." She said it almost bitterly and pushed back
her chair. "Everything's fine, isn't it?"

He raised an eyebrow. "Did I say that?"

"No." She gave an apologetic shrug. "I'm just in a lousy
mood. I'm sorry, Jonny. Forget it, will you?"

He followed her out of the restaurant. A hint of rain was

in the air and the first few drops began falling as they reached the cars.

"You go on your own," said Anna suddenly. "I feel like doing some sight-seeing—the cathedral maybe, and there are a couple of other guide-book places."

"I'll come along if you want," said Gaunt.

She shook her head. "Another time. Right now I'd be better alone and I'll make you a promise. I'll try to be in a better mood afterwards."

He nodded and left her.

Getting out of Troyes wasn't too easy, but before long Gaunt was driving south on the main N.71 route, a level road running through the upper valley of the Seine.

After fifteen minutes the rain really began falling—no romantic grey misting but a heavy, battering torrent which almost overwhelmed the screenwipers, flooded in long shallow pools across the road, and cut visibility in a way that reduced most of the traffic to a near crawl. With only about two hundred kilometres to go to the next overnight stop, Gaunt could afford to take it easy, but some of the heavy commercial traffic kept thundering on, throwing bow-waves of rain water as they passed, almost drowning some of the inevitable little Citroen 2 C.V.s which kept cluttering the roads.

The rain lasted half an hour, then stopped, and the sky cleared. Some tourist cars began pulling in for picnics, a long French army convoy trundled past him heading north, and the flat countryside gradually began to give way to low, gently wooded hills.

The tempting sight of a bar and restaurant appeared ahead and he slowed, then saw the car park and changed his mind. The black B.M.W. and Hubbard and Dawson's blue Saab were there, parked side by side, and for the moment the last thing he wanted to do was to appear inquisitive in that direction.

A few kilometres on, he almost regretted it. The Corran family's Ford station wagon was drawn in at the verge and Frank Corran was trying to change a wheel.

Gaunt stopped and helped Corran struggle with his antiquated jack and a wheel-brace that barely managed to cope with the rusted wheel-nuts. The job took half an hour, including the cup of coffee which Maggie Corran brewed on a bottled-gas stove while they worked.

"The damned tyre just blew on us in the middle of that rainstorm," said Corran, stowing his tool-kit away. "Hell, it was long enough before I could even get out of the car to have a look at it." He scowled at the balding spare now in place. "That one isn't much good, but as long as it gets us to the motel for tonight and I can find a garage, who cares?"

"I'd take it easy," advised Gaunt.

"Easy?" Corran thumbed towards the back of the station wagon, where his young son sat happily tearing a comic book to shreds. "Look, I don't need a speedometer. Fifty miles an hour and he gets car-sick. At sixty, Maggie starts on about my life insurance. Go over that, and the steering goes to hell anyway."

"Because we need a new car," said Maggie Corran pointedly. "I'm not worried about getting to Switzerland. It's whether we'll get back again that really jangles me."

"You can always get out and push," said Corran. "Exercise, Maggie—it's good for the figure."

Gaunt left them discussing exactly who needed exercise

most, got back into the Chrysler, and started driving again. Within five minutes he saw another Safari car, the Walkers' green coupe, stopped outside a roadside café.

It was another few kilometres on before he gradually realised he had company, a big white Citroen which stayed well back, little more than a dot in his rear-view mirror. Gaunt overtook a few cars, was passed by a couple of snarling Japanese motorcycles, and saw the Citroen was still there.

At first, it was only a bored experiment. He slowed, and the white car behind first reduced the gap then dropped back again. Gently, interested now, Gaunt increased the Chrysler's speed again and watched. The car behind kept pace.

Swearing to himself, he waited until the next straight stretch of road then deliberately pulled in and stopped, waiting. Seconds ticked past on the dashboard clock then the Citroen swept past him and he sighed at his own stupidity.

It was a private ambulance, a white-coated driver at the wheel, blinds drawn and Red Cross badges on its side panels.

After that, he just drove with the car radio turned to a French station that was mercifully pumping out jazz instead of pop.

Winding through a series of deep river valleys, the road emerged at the sprawling, unexpectedly large city of Dijon, which the guide books rated as a cultural centre. But he didn't feel interested in art galleries or old Burgundian palaces, so he stuck with the through route and emerged in hilly, vineyard country studded with roadside stalls ready to sell the local product by the glass or the tanker-load.

Gaunt bought a bottle of *ordinaire* for a few francs with

Harry Falconer in mind, then kept going. Ten minutes later he passed a road sign for Parcy; soon after that the Chrysler reached the Motel Hirondelle, journey's end for the day.

He drove through a tall concrete arch topped by a cast-bronze swallow with outspread wings, stopped in the car park which fronted the Hirondelle, and got out thankfully.

Several other cars were lying in the paint-outlined spaces around. One was the white Citroen ambulance. The rear door was open and it was empty. Mrs. MacLean's and Miss Stewart's green Fiat station wagon sat two spaces along, the polished paintwork spattered with mud and a new mascot, a small toy race-horse, dangling at the rear window. As he passed, he noticed several bottles of wine laid in a neat precision along the Fiat's back shelf.

The two retired schoolteachers seemed to be making the most of their trip. He shrugged, remembering the Safari was supposed to be a tourist outing, and turned towards the motel.

The lay-out was single-storey and shaped like a bull's head. Administration offices, restaurant, and a bar formed the middle section with a curved horn of motel rooms sweeping out on either side. Between the horns was a strip of garden, a small swimming pool, and an open-air café, with several guests drifting around the area.

He checked in at the reception office where a tall, slim girl with raven-black hair ticked his name on her list.

"*Appartement dix-sept*, M'sieu Gaunt . . . seventeen," she said with a friendly smile. "Enjoy your stay."

Gaunt took the key she slid across the counter, then indicated the mail rack behind her.

"Any messages for me?" he asked casually.

She glanced at the rack, then shook her head.

"If one comes I'd like to know." He leaned against the counter, chose and paid for a couple of postcards from a display shelf, then used that as an opener. "Why the ambulance outside? Someone hurt?"

"Here, m'sieu?" She sounded slightly indignant at the suggestion. "No, it is taking a patient back to Switzerland from Paris, a M'sieu Phillipe who was injured in a road accident."

"Just a driver with him?" queried Gaunt.

"A friend also accompanies him," she shrugged sympathetically. "M'sieu Phillipe's legs are injured, so he needs help."

The telephone rang and she turned away to answer it. Picking up his overnight bag, Gaunt left her and located apartment seventeen halfway down one of the horns of the building. It was a compact, comfortably furnished twin-bedded room with a shower and toilet, coin-in-slot TV, and a pay-as-you-use drinks cabinet. One wall had a large crack in the plaster from floor to ceiling, but it looked as though it had been there for a long time.

Dumping the overnight bag, he tried the nearest bed, found the mattress hard the way he liked them, then freshened himself at the washbasin. Drying the water from his face with one of the motel's sky-blue towels, he lit a cigarette and decided to explore.

Outside, the scent of the pine wood in his nostrils, he was crossing the little strip of garden when he heard his name being called from the café tables beside the pool. Two elderly, bird-like faces beamed a welcome as he went over.

"Like some coffee, Mr. Gaunt?" asked Miss Stewart cheerfully, gesturing to the pot beside her.

"He'd rather have a drink," said Mrs. MacLean firmly. "Wouldn't you?"

"Coffee sounds fine," said Gaunt, taking the vacant seat beside them. "Well, what have you two been up to today? The back of your car looks like a travelling bar."

Miss Stewart made a sound suspiciously like a giggle. He suddenly realised that Mrs. MacLean was slightly owl-eyed as she beckoned the waitress to bring another cup.

"We stopped at those vineyard places," said Miss Stewart. She shook her head in a slight bewilderment. "We just seemed to keep sampling drinks and buying bottles. It—"

"It left us slightly stoned," said Mrs. MacLean. The fresh cup came and she filled it with coffee from the pot, using both hands to keep the flow steady. "Do we look stoned, Mr. Gaunt?"

"No," he assured them. "Just—uh—pleased."

"Two retired schoolteachers from St. Andrews." Miss Stewart giggled again. "Elsie, I don't think the neighbours would approve back home."

Mrs. MacLean snorted. "The neighbours can get knotted." She beamed at Gaunt. "If you'll pardon the expression. Some of my pupils used to use it."

He grinned. "Where'd you get the horse mascot?"

"Brought it with us," said Miss Stewart. "But we didn't like to put it up till now. That's Sierra Sue"—her small face crinkled earnestly—"the horse's name, I mean, Mr. Gaunt. She's a very special horse. Mary, can't we tell him?"

"We'd better, now," sighed Mrs. MacLean. She leaned

across the table confidentially. "Sierra Sue is a race-horse, Mr. Gaunt—the reason we're here. Do you know about betting?"

"A little," he admitted solemnly.

"Do you know what a three-cross roll-up double is?" asked Miss Stewart sharply.

Gaunt blinked. "A hell of a long-shot gamble, for the professionals."

"That's what Michael, our milkman back home, told us," agreed Mrs. MacLean. "But he was trying one—"

"Then I'd just got this insurance policy money, two hundred pounds, and Elsie and I were discussing what to do with it," chipped in Miss Stewart. "I mean, two hundred pounds now—it would hardly get you a decent burial."

"You mean you put it on the horses?" Gaunt stared at them. They nodded cheerfully.

"On Michael's three-cross thing," said Mrs. MacLean. "All on the one afternoon, Mr. Gaunt. Sierra Sue was the last horse of all and—and"—she beamed at him—"and we cleared almost ten thousand pounds."

"Except we can't let the neighbours know," said Miss Stewart earnestly. "I mean, we're churchgoers, and Elsie's treasurer of the organ fund. You understand, don't you?"

"They'll never hear from me," promised Gaunt with a straight face. "So this trip is your celebration?"

The two women looked at each other and nodded happily.

"To Sierra Sue, then," said Gaunt, raising his coffee cup in a toast. "But don't ever try it agan." He shook his head warningly. "That might make you professionals."

He sat back, with a feeling that one car would now be removed from his list.

The rest of the Safari Suisse group were among the cars that drifted into the Motel Hirondelle over the next hour or so. Most of the time, Gaunt watched the arrivals from the bar. He'd gone there after leaving Sierra Sue's two elderly fans and, with a beer in front of him, it made as good a vantage point as any.

The Corrans came first, Frank Corran installing his wife and child in their room then driving off in search of a garage to have his tyre repaired. Hubbard and Dawson were next with the Saab, checked in, and went to a room on the apartment horn opposite Gaunt's. Five minutes later, an unexpected surprise, the black B.M.W. rolled in and the tall, bearded driver also took a room for the night.

That was enough to take Gaunt down from his bar stool and through to the reception office. He made some lonely tourist chat with the raven-haired receptionist, who seemed glad of the diversion, and returned to the bar with most of what he wanted to know.

The B.M.W.'s owner was Henry Boisson, who was travelling on a Swiss passport and had registered with a Montreux address. The passport described him as a company director and he had apartment number six—a long way from Hubbard and Dawson. At the same time, Gaunt had collected another apartment number. Carl Phillipe, the injured man from the ambulance, had number forty, which was big enough to sleep three.

Another half hour passed. Hubbard and Dawson appeared and had drinks at the open-air tables. Then Henry

Boisson, a tanned, muscular figure wearing only swimming trunks and carrying a towel, emerged briefly, took a plunge into the pool and went back to his room. There was no sign of movement from number forty.

Moments after Boisson had returned to his room the last two Safari Suisse cars rolled in almost together. The Walkers arrived first, their Ford coupe travel-stained like the others but with a smashed headlamp glass and a dented radiator grille. Behind them, Anna Hart brought her little Triumph smartly through the lines of cars and tucked it into another parking place.

Going out, Gaunt was in time to see Mary Walker, her round face stonier than ever, lead the way towards the reception office with her husband limping his customary few steps behind. Hubbard rose from his chair at the open-air tables, wandered over to talk to them for a moment, then ambled back and joined Dawson again.

Anna had the hood folded down on the Triumph and was fitting a black plastic tonneau cover in place when Gaunt reached her.

"Much longer, and I'd have been organising a search party," he said amiably. "How did the sight-seeing go?"

"All right." She fastened the last couple of tonneau studs, used a hand to comb back her long, tousled hair, and gave him a wry smile. "And—well, I got rid of that mood, then decided I'd rejoin the human race."

"That helps." He winked at her. "Welcome back. Any idea how the Walkers dented their car?"

She shook her head.

"Well, we'll hear." He stooped to lift her overnight case.

"I'll help you book in—though it's going to ruin my prospects at the reception desk."

"Wait, Jonny." She laid a hand on his arm. "I bought a newspaper back at Troyes."

"So?" He raised an eyebrow.

"A man was found murdered at Villiers this morning," she said gravely. Producing a torn piece of newsprint from the top pocket of her denim jacket, she smoothed it out. "I thought you'd want to know."

Face expressionless, Gaunt took the torn section of newspaper and read his way through the brief, factual report. The dead man had been found caught up against rocks in a stretch of the river just below Villiers at day-break. His body had stab wounds in the chest and his identity was unknown.

"An earlier outbreak of violence between local people and *les militares* from a nearby army camp is regarded by police as significant," said the report hopefully. "All army units at the camp are confined to barracks while investigations continue."

But the final few lines hit Gaunt hardest. The dead man had been young and small, with sharp features. He had been wearing a dark sweatshirt and slacks.

Just like the man he'd stumbled across in the courtyard of the Hotel Le Duc. The man who had vanished in the brief period when Gaunt had been knocked out.

"Nasty," he said slowly, folding the piece of newsprint and handing it back. "Are you trying to say it could have been me?"

"Yes. That's part of it." Earnestly, she touched his arm

again. "Jonny, was there anything more to what happened last night—anything more than you told me?"

"Should there have been?" he asked obliquely, then deliberately shook his head and lied. "No, it just leaves me feeling lucky."

She looked puzzled for a moment, vaguely disappointed, then nodded reluctantly. He picked up the overnight bag and started with her to the reception office.

The front-end dent in the Walkers' car had happened when Mary Walker hit a cow, one of a milking herd straggling across the road as the green Ford coupe had rounded a bend.

"The cow only got a bruised backside, but it cost the Walkers a hundred francs to soothe the farmer." Maggie Corran grinned unsympathetically. "She's as mad as hell about it—the Walker woman I mean. I don't know about the cow."

The Corrans had turned up for a drink at the open-air tables before dinner, leaving their four-year-old more or less asleep in their room. Gaunt and Anna had arrived about the same time and Frank Corran had insisted on buying the round.

"Call it thanks for helping me with that tyre," he said as he paid, pushing Gaunt's money aside. "You know what Maggie wants me to do? Go up to Madame Walker and say 'moo.' But no way—she'd probably break my neck for starters."

"Maybe that was the idea," murmured Anna. She nudged Gaunt. "Would you do it?"

"No," said Gaunt absently. "I've talked to her husband."

He let the talk flow round him, watching apartment forty across the way. A waiter from the Hirondelle's restaurant had just delivered a tray of food to the door and the man who had taken it was the ambulance driver, the only one of the three occupants who had so far shown himself since Gaunt had arrived.

The apartment door closed, the waiter left, and a figure appeared briefly at the apartment window, closing the curtains. A moment later, light showed round the edges of the window in the gathering dusk. Number forty's trio obviously intended to maintain their privacy.

He glanced at Anna. Like the others, she had stayed in her travelling clothes but any hint of her earlier tiredness after the day's drive had gone. Her eyes sparkled as she laughed at an involved joke Corran told about an American tourist and a Scotsman and his kilt.

It was the old pay-off line, that nothing was worn under the kilt—everything was in perfect working order. He gave an obligatory grin but was glad when the Corrans decided they'd check that their young son was sleeping and left.

He went with Anna to the restaurant a couple of minutes later and they were given a window table for two. The meal, when it came, was ordinary motel-style deep-freeze cooking but they were both hungry enough not to care.

He lit a cigarette for Anna between courses, took one for himself, then looked round. One surprise that interested him was that the Walkers were sharing a table with Hubbard and Dawson, with Mary Walker apparently enjoying it and her husband having a low-voiced, earnest conversation with Dawson. Two tables away, the bearded man called Boisson was sitting by himself, picking with some distaste at the food in front of him, sipping a glass of wine, and apparently ignoring his surroundings.

Except that, suddenly, Hubbard got up, excused himself, and headed for the men's room. When he came back after a minute his route took him past Boisson's table. The two men exchanged a glance, Boisson gave a slight, negative headshake, and Hubbard rejoined the others.

Whatever existed between the two men from the Saab, they clearly had no intention of bringing it out in the open. There was a dead man back at Villiers who might have known, but who else?

His glance strayed to the Walkers again, from there to where the Corrans were sharing a table with a German couple. And, finally, to Anna.

She smiled as their eyes met. It didn't help a bit.

CHAPTER 4

Crickets were chirping in the shadows of the motel garden when they left the restaurant. The moon was out, the sky almost clear of cloud and sprinkled with stars, and the wind was little more than a cool breeze rustling in through the pine trees.

"How far tomorrow?" asked Anna quietly.

"Three hours driving, maybe less." Gaunt nodded towards the east. "The Swiss frontier is only about a hundred kilometres from here. Anybody really keen could make Montreaux tonight."

Or do the whole trip from the Channel ports in a single day of hard, determined driving. His lips twisted sardonically at the thought that by air the whole thing was maybe a couple of hours.

Beside him, Anne looked round. Some of the motel apartments were already in darkness and even the bar wasn't doing much trade. She gave a soft sound like a sigh.

"Penny for it," suggested Gaunt.

"What I was thinking?" Anna shook her head. "It isn't worth that much, Jonny." She drew a deep breath. "Mind if we walk for a little?"

There was a path from the motel garden up through the pine trees. They stopped in a clearing near the top, the view out towards the long, brooding silhouette of the Jura

Mountains with Switzerland beyond the dark ridges. Perhaps it was a trick of the moonlight, but he had an impression of white-capped peaks in the far distance.

"This time tomorrow—" he began.

Anna stopped him. "Don't, Jonny. I—well, I don't believe in planning ahead any more." She paused, then added in a wistful voice. "But I'm glad you're here."

"That makes two of us," he said gravely. He put an arm round her shoulders and felt her shiver. "Cold?"

She shook her head, then suddenly, almost fiercely, turned towards him. Their lips met eagerly, he felt the warmth of her body against his own, and in the same instant each instinctively knew and shared the other's long-stored need and longing in a way that excluded all else.

There was a grassy bank just under the shelter of the pine trees. It welcomed them and they needed nothing more.

It was after midnight when they walked, hand in hand, down the path through the trees to the Motel Hirondelle. A single light still burned outside the reception office, but the other buildings were in darkness and only the crickets broke the silence.

Gaunt stopped as they reached Anna's apartment door, smiled down at her, then kissed her gently.

"Jonny." She held on to his hand. "I meant what I said. I don't plan ahead. But—"

"Well?" He made to kiss her again but stopped when she shook her head.

"I'm glad," she said softly. "More than you know."

Then, very quickly, she turned away, unlocked the apartment door, and went inside. The door closed again, quietly, and Gaunt stayed where he was for a long minute before he turned away.

The crickets were still chirping and the scent of the pines remained in the wind. He felt a sense of peace, the kind that hadn't come often in the last couple of years. As for tomorrow, he went along with Anna. It could wait.

Gaunt stopped halfway across the garden, on the way to his own apartment, and turned to glance back at her door. Instead, he spotted a faint glimmer of light over at the motel parking lot—and switched back to instant, instinctive reality.

The light vanished then showed again, a wavering glow as if someone was using a shielded hand-torch. Taking to the grass verge, keeping to the darker shadows of the garden, Gaunt headed silently in its direction. As he went, he realised the glow was coming from about the middle of the fourth row of cars.

From the edge of the garden to the first row was a few quick, tip-toed strides, then he hugged the shelter of a Volkswagen for a moment. The glow of light went out then came on again, along the fourth row as before and three or four cars to his right.

A voice cursed softly, the sound carrying in the still night air. Then he heard a grunt and a rustle and the figure of a man showed briefly in the glow, only to vanish again while the glow moved in an oddly cut-off way.

Someone had a very keen interest in the underside of that particular car. Gaunt eased forward to the next line of vehicles, hugged cold metal again, then shifted his position slightly to get a better view.

The car he was against had an exterior mirror on the driver's door. As he moved, he caught another flicker of movement in its glass, a movement from somewhere behind and to his left. He froze, then deliberately moved across the gap to the next car, this time watching the faint, moonlit reflection in the window glass.

The same flicker of movement repeated itself. So he had company, and the man with the torch wasn't alone. Something else registered in a way he didn't like. The new arrival, if he was standing sentry, appeared to have no intention of warning his companion. Meaning he intended to handle any interruption on his own.

Except Gaunt had played the same kind of game before, with experts, when he'd worn a uniform. Flopping down on the dusty ground, he rolled quickly across the space to the next car in line and stopped when he was hidden under it. His fingers searched quickly for a stone or gravel then closed on something even better, an old, crushed beer can.

Wriggling round, he lobbed the beer can out on the far side of the car. It landed softly but clearly, then he hugged the ground again and waited.

Long moments passed, then he heard a quiet pad of feet. The man reached the car and stopped beside it, only his legs visible as he leaned against the bodywork. He had suede ankle-length boots, buckle-fastened, and Gaunt heard him murmur a curse as he tried to locate his quarry again.

Tensing, Gaunt counted to three. Then he came out from under the car in a ground-level dive, tackling him round the ankles with one arm, the sheer surprise as much as impetus throwing the man off balance and dragging him down.

Immediately, Gaunt knew he was dealing with a pro—and a good one, at least his match in build and strength. His opponent didn't cry out or panic. A grunt as he hit the ground, then the left arm was up fending Gaunt off while the right swung in a tight, chopping arc.

Gaunt jerked his head sideways in time. The faint moonlight glinted momentarily on the barrel of a silencer-fitted automatic, then the intended pistol-whip blow grazed past him and slammed the dirt as they rolled and grappled.

The silent struggle went on, and their bodies slammed against one of the car's wheels. The man, his face a mere vague outline in the night, panted and snarled, then they rolled again in the dirt. Gaunt tried to change his grip, caught the stranger's jacket, and cloth ripped.

It was the chance the other man had needed. For a moment he was on top, his free hand chopped sideways at Gaunt's neck, and he broke free. Clenched teeth a white grimace, he brought the gun round again, finger tightening on the trigger.

But it was Gaunt's chance too. He gave a twisting half-roll which was an old parachute-landing technique, then kicked upward. His heel pistoned against the point of his opponent's elbow with jarring, bone-shattering force which brought a high-pitched squeal of pain. The man fell backwards, the gun falling from his suddenly paralysed fingers, then he stumbled to his feet whimpering, and turned to run.

Gaunt scrambled up, starting after him—then just as

quickly flopped down again at the soft report of a silenced pistol and the sound of a bullet smacking the ground near his feet.

He rolled under the nearest car as the silencer plopped again and a torch beam swept where he'd been moments before. The second man had come to his look-out's aid.

Voices muttered, the torch swung again, and he rolled out on the other side of the car, kept going under the next car and the next again, then stopped and lay silent, hugging the ground, his heart thumping, panting for breath.

He heard footsteps and the mutter of voices kept on. The torch beam had gone out and the two men seemed to be having an angry, low-voiced argument.

Then, suddenly, there was silence.

Gaunt lay motionless for a full five minutes while his breathing steadied and the hard ground grew more uncomfortable. At last, cautiously, he wriggled out into the open again and got to his feet.

The men had gone. For the first time, he realised his back muscles were aching from unaccustomed strain. Grinning a little in the night, he decided it wasn't too much of a price to pay. The man with the smashed elbow would probably have agreed.

Still cautious but curious, he went over to where he'd first seen the man with the torch. Then his lips shaped a silent whistle of interest. The car was the Walkers' green Ford coupe, still with its dented front grille and smashed headlamp.

His back stabbing in a way that made him grimace, Gaunt wriggled under the Ford's tail and risked using the tiny flame of his cigarette lighter. The car was under-sealed, but a long, narrow flap of the protective, rubbery compound had been partially cut away near one of the rear-wheel arches. Which meant he'd interrupted a determined search for possible cut-and-weld hiding places.

The Customs man at Dover had claimed a real search virtually amounted to taking a car to pieces. But the raw cut was there, and it confirmed so many other things that had gone before.

He wasn't the only outsider who knew that the Safari Suisse party was being used as cover for a currency smuggling operation. But if a hi-jacking move was planned, it still seemed the men behind it weren't totally certain which car was their target. Grimly, he added the one other fact he knew. They were ready to kill whenever necessary.

Wriggling out again, Caunt walked back to the spot where he'd had that brief, vicious struggle.

The gun the injured man had dropped was gone. A few scrape marks on the ground around showed where they'd rolled and fought.

Shrugging, he started to turn away, then saw a thin streamer of white lying half under the front wheels of the nearest car. Stopping, he picked up a grubby handkerchief and, as he did, some loose coins fell from its folds.

So did something else, a book of Motel Hirondelle matches. He stared at them, then swore softly, remembering how the man's jacket had torn. Squatting down beside the wheel, he used his lighter again and spotted a crushed pack of French cigarettes. But just beside them, glinting in the tiny, flickering flame, lay a set of car keys.

Keys attached to a Citroen car fob. Nursing the keys and the Hirondelle book matches in his hand, he rose and looked around for the white Citroen ambulance. It was at the far end of the parking lot and he rubbed the keys between his fingers for a moment, then made up his mind and went there.

The first key he tried slid smoothly into the ambulance's door lock and clicked it open.

That was all he wanted to know. As soon as the keys were missed, the alleged patient and his two companions holed up in apartment forty would come looking for them.

Gaunt locked the ambulance door again, then paused.

"What the hell?" he said softly, with a grin at the moon.

It took seconds to scoop up a couple of handfuls of dirt, pour them down the ambulance's fuel filler pipe, and replace the cap.

Then he went back, dropped the keys where he'd found them, and started for the motel. Not through the garden this time, because he was certain the men in apartment forty would be on watch.

Five minutes later, after forcing the snib on the rear window, he climbed into his own room. Closing the window again, suddenly tired and his back aching, he reached the bed, slumped down on it, and kicked off his shoes.

He slept that way, and the parachute nightmare came once but, blurred and vaguely unreal, was crowded into the background by too much else.

Sunlight was streaming in through the room window when Gaunt wakened again. Yawning, he glanced at his wristwatch and winced when he saw it was 10 A.M. That brought him wide awake, then, with a grimace at his sleep-crumpled clothes, he stretched carefully on the bed.

His back felt stiff, but nothing more. Relieved, he frowned up at the ceiling for a moment. The last day of the run—if a hi-jack operation was under way, and that seemed obvious now, when and where was it likely to happen?

He sucked his teeth over that one. Suppose the half-million in currency was hidden in the Walker's car, then what? He frowned again at the ceiling and corrected that. Suppose the hi-jackers weren't sure, were trying to narrow down to a final choice just as he was doing? Then they might wait until Montreaux itself and make their play right under the noses of the money-laundry operators.

It made the most sense and he settled for it hopefully. Getting up, pulling on his shoes, he washed and shaved and only then noticed that a note had been pushed under his door.

Collecting the single sheet, he read it with mixed feelings.

JONNY. MAYBE TOMORROWS DO MATTER LIKE LAST NIGHT DID. BUT I'M ON MY WAY. SEE YOU IN SWITZ. ANNA.

Slowly, deliberately, he tore the note up and dropped it into the waste bucket. What had happened between them was something too real for him to want to even try to explore. Not yet, not as long as he still didn't know what lay ahead—or whether the dark-haired girl was part of it all. And the continued lack of word from John Milton in Edinburgh was becoming ominous.

He shrugged at himself in the mirror, lit a cigarette, and went out to get breakfast. The sun was warm, a last trace of early morning mist was wisping away from the slopes above, and the cars in the parking lot had already thinned to a fraction of their overnight number. But the white Citroen ambulance was still there.

Glancing across at apartment forty, he slowed. The door lay open and had a suitcase lying beside it. He took another look at the parking lot, saw the ambulance starting to move, and stayed where he was with the cigarette dangling from his lips and hopefully giving the impression of a man enjoying the sunlight.

Moving at a crawl, the ambulance came along the line of motel rooms, stopped outside number forty with the engine running, and the white-coated driver got out. He opened the rear door of the ambulance, loaded the suitcase aboard, then went inside number forty.

When the driver reappeared, he was pushing a lightweight wheelchair. The man in it was young, mousey-haired, long-jawed, and had his legs covered by a rug. Behind them came the third man, a stockily built, sullen-faced individual who had his right arm in a sling. As the little procession reached the rear of the ambulance, Gaunt flicked his cigarette away and strolled over.

"Need any help?" he asked.

"*Mais non* . . . thank you, but we can manage," said the man in the wheelchair stonily.

"If you're sure." Gaunt made a sympathetic noise. "When I saw that your friend had hurt his arm—"

"Just a little, a strain." The man in the wheelchair forced a smile while his two companions stayed silent, tight-lipped. He had a pair of the coldest blue eyes Gaunt had ever seen. "We can still manage, m'sieu—"

"Gaunt." Innocently, Gaunt leaned against the ambulance door. "Travelling much further, M'sieu Phillipe?"

The long-jawed face hardened. "Why?"

"The girl at reception said you were on your way home, after some kind of road accident." Gaunt shrugged. "Can't be too comfortable a way to travel."

"We haven't far to go." Phillipe glanced at the ambulance driver and nodded. "Excuse us, m'sieu."

Gaunt stood back while the wheelchair manoeuvred, then Phillipe, aided by his companions, levered himself into the ambulance. In the process, the man with the sling bumped his arm against the bodywork and gave a startled grunt of pain. Face suddenly a pasty grey, the man waited until Phillipe was on the ambulance bunk then lurched in beside him and sat down. Quickly, the driver folded the wheelchair and tucked it aboard.

"Safe journey," Gaunt said cheerfully.

"*Merci* . . . and to you," answered Phillipe. His cold blue eyes didn't blink. "It pays to be careful, m'sieu. Accidents can happen to anyone—anytime."

The rear door closed and the driver got in behind the wheel. As the ambulance drove away, Gaunt combed a hand through his hair and his freckled, raw-boned face shaped a grin.

They weren't sure who had tangled with them in that night darkness. They might suspect him, but they weren't sure—not even the man with the sling, who looked as though he needed a doctor's care.

In a cheerful mood, Gaunt kicked a pebble along in front of him as he walked over to the restaurant. Inside, the place was almost empty and the girl who served him a coffee and rolls breakfast at a window seat made it plain she didn't approve of latecomers.

Soon afterwards he heard car engines and glanced up. Two Safari Suisse cars were leaving the parking lot—the Walkers in their Ford and the blue Saab with Hubbard and Dawson aboard. As Gaunt watched, the Ford was first to go out through the Hirondelle's concrete archway with the Saab slotting into place behind it like an escort.

He almost choked on the coffee he'd been sipping. An escort—he should have had sense to realise it long before. Hubbard and Dawson, the rank outsiders, could simply be along to see that the currency consignment got through this time.

He stared as the Saab vanished beyond the archway, remembering the other blue Saab that had been mangled by a truck that didn't stop, then the man who had been killed at Villiers the night before. It was as if he'd been a spectator on the edge of a small, secret war.

"May I join you, M'sieu Gaunt?" asked a lazy voice.

Taken off guard, he turned. The tall, bearded Henry Boisson was standing beside his table.

"You don't mind?" Boisson slipped into the chair opposite without waiting for an answer. He wore a checked wool shirt and grey whipcord slacks, and a pair of driving glasses in a leather case peeped from his shirt pocket. "I'd like to talk to you for a minute."

"About what?" Gaunt raised a deliberate eyebrow.

"Something I hope will interest you." Casually Boisson waved away the waitress as she started to come over. "I ate earlier, but when I saw you here I couldn't think of a better opportunity. You see, I—ah—want to make you an offer, M'sieu Gaunt."

"If it's anything that costs money you're wasting your time," said Gaunt sardonically. Every instinct he possessed was screaming caution. Since the first time he'd seen Boisson, back at that village fairground, he'd known the bearded man probably mattered more than anyone else in the whole mad chase. "But go on— I'm in no hurry."

"*Merci.*" The man nodded, unabashed. "I'm a Swiss, M'sieu Gaunt—my name is Henry Boisson, the first part because my mother was English. Right now, I'm on my way home to Montreux, where I have a garage business and—ah—other interests. Then, when I met some of your Safari Suisse group here and heard you were all heading for Montreux, I had an idea."

"Like turning round and going away again?" suggested Gaunt.

Boisson chuckled. "How would you like your car fully serviced at half normal cost—a special discount?"

"Why?" Gaunt looked puzzled, which was how he felt. He picked up a spoon and used its tip to draw a pattern on the tablecloth. "Is there a catch, or are you just feeling benevolent?"

"Neither. But a wise driver would always have his car serviced after a long journey." Boisson reached into his shirt pocket and placed a slip of pasteboard in front of Gaunt. "I have made the same offer to the other Safari people. The garage is Automobiles Tamboure— show them this, and they'll do the rest."

"And what do you get out of it?" asked Gaunt dryly, picking up the card.

"A good advertising promotion, the kind the oil companies admire." Boisson lazed back in his chair. "The offer is good anytime over the next couple of days. What do you say?"

"That I like saving money." Gaunt gave a slow nod. "Been away from home long?"

"A few days," said Boisson easily. "I was in Holland on business till yesterday, then started driving back. By the time I reached here, I decided I had come far enough in one day. But it's time I got started again." He pushed back his chair, rose, then paused. "One small thing, while I remember. I saw you talking to those people with the ambulance. Do you know them?"

Gaunt shook his head. "They just looked like they needed help, but they didn't."

"Had you seen them before?"

"No." Gaunt eyed the man.

Boisson shrugged. "Some strange people travel this road. You should be careful who you speak to along the way." His beard split in a white-toothed grin. "Foreigners, M'sieu Gaunt. You can't trust them."

Then he left.

Balancing the garage card between his fingers, Gaunt sat motionless for a moment and felt a grudging admiration for the man's cool nerve and the clever simplicity of the servicing offer.

It meant any, probably every, car in the Safari would roll into that one garage. Where the car with the currency consignment could be worked on without any questions being asked.

But Boisson had still been careless. He'd lied about coming direct from Holland. He'd pushed his luck a little in asking about the Citroen ambulance—which meant in turn that he was suspicious in that direction, warily on his guard. Gaunt chuckled a little. Anyone with half a million pounds in currency riding across Europe was entitled to feel that way, even without a hi-jack threat in the foreground.

His breakfast coffee had gone cold. He ordered a fresh pot, lit a cigarette, and stayed in the restaurant until he'd seen the Swiss drive off in the black B.M.W.

Then, and only then, he decided it was time to leave.

From the Motel Hirondelle the road to the frontier began to climb and twist a way through the wooded mountains. It was a busy road, thick with tourist traffic and heavy trucks, studded with warning signs and guard rails, and Gaunt found he could do little more than keep the Chrysler purring along with the rest of the flow while the sun shone down and the engine temperature gauge rose a few notches in protest.

About thirty kilometres on, he reached a village—and saw something which made him chuckle and forget the heat as he drove through.

The Citroen ambulance was stopped outside the village garage, the engine hood up and a mechanic working under it. There was no sign of the Citroen's occupants, but he could imagine their feelings. The two handfuls of dirt he'd added to the fuel tank must have done nasty things to the Citroen's carburation long before they got that distance and it was going to take time before they were on the road again.

The route kept climbing. For a time the trees gave way to a rocky, desolate stretch of high country but that gave way again to thickly wooded slopes. Here and there he spotted a chalet perched high above the road and the brown cattle grazing in the handkerchief-sized fields had bells around their necks.

It was just before noon when he reached the frontier near Vallorbe. On the French side, that meant a perfunctory passport check. A stone's throw on, the Swiss frontier guard didn't even bother to leave his hut and waved him through.

Gaunt stopped at a café and filling station just beyond, where the red and white Swiss flag flew above a list of recognised credit cards. He topped up the car, changed his French money for Swiss francs, took time off for a beer and a plate of veal stew, then got under way again.

Still climbing, the narrow road wound through mountain scenery which would have caught and held him on any ordinary trip. But Gaunt felt impatient now and pushed on, glad when the mountains gave way again to lower farming land and he could build up speed on the broadening highway.

Even so, he did slow when he topped a final rise of ground and had his first view of the tourist playground on ahead.

Like a vast, calm, blue sea, Lake Geneva was spread in front of him with a backcloth of distant, occasionally snow-capped mountains. Tiny white lake steamers were moving across it, threading between even smaller sailboats. Lausanne was a sunlit lake-edge city not many kilometres on—

and just in front of him was an autoroute direction sign which included the magic word "Montreux."

Minutes later he was on the multi-lane highway and enjoying the feel of being able to give the Chrysler its head. The snarling traffic round had registration plates from all over Europe and North America, and, Swiss style, the autoroute engineers had treated nature with scant respect. At times the highway appeared suspended from sheer rock, at other moments it dived through tunnels—with the bright blue of Lake Geneva never far away to the right.

It was early afternoon when he entered Montreux and drove along the lakeside to the town centre. Stopping beside a policewoman on points duty, he asked the way to the Hotel Julien.

She was pretty, she was blonde, she wore an outfit of powder blue with a white blouse and pillbox hat, and even the small, holstered automatic resting on her smooth curve of hip didn't seem wrong.

"From here, m'sieu?" She looked Gaunt over with a twinkling, unprofessional interest. "*Un moment . . .*"

A boy on a motorcycle was coming along. She stopped him, spoke briefly, and came back.

"He will show you, m'sieu," she said demurely. "Enjoy your stay."

The motorcyclist didn't have to take him far. A few streets on they parted with a wave and Gaunt parked in the underground garage beneath the Hotel Julien.

The Julien was on the lakeside, like the brochures claimed. It was also big, modern, multi-storey, and had the kind of lobby carpet that looked as though it would be cut with a lawnmower. From the reception desk, a porter took Gaunt and his luggage by elevator to the eighth floor and along to a room which had a single bed, built-in furniture, and not much floor space. He had a window which led onto a postage-stamp balcony with a view towards the lake and there was a small shower-room and toilet.

There were two telegram envelopes lying propped against the dressing-table mirror. Tipping the porter, locking the door once the man had gone, Gaunt ripped open the envelopes.

The first, from John Milton in Edinburgh, left him exasperated. All it said was "PHONE ME DIRECTLY URGENTLIEST." Milton counted his pennies when it came to non-essential chat.

But the second left him pondering uneasily, his previous good humour wiped away. The Queen's and Lord Treasurer's Remembrancer's office could be equally brief when it mattered. "CONTACT YOUR LOCAL FRIENDS ON ARRIVAL. FALCONER." was a total contradiction of his earlier instruction that the Montreux contacts were for emergencies only.

He burned both telegrams, flushed the ashes away in the little washroom, then used the bedside telephone and made Edinburgh his first priority. The hotel switchboard placed a direct-dial call for him straightaway and in under a minute John Milton was at the other end of a line which had a soft background quota of squealing harmonics.

"So you got there," said Milton over the squealing. "God, this line's as bad as a local call. God trip?"

"It would have been better if I'd heard from you earlier," said Gaunt stonily. "Like two days ago, the way we arranged."

He heard the Edinburgh stockbroker give an indignant grunt.

"To hell with you too," answered Milton, unperturbed. "If you didn't owe me so much money, I'd hang up."

"Point taken," agreed Gaunt. "All right, I'll start again. But I've got problems."

"Like those two thousand Rhuvalla shares I've got you," said Milton with a sadistic cheerfulness. "Against my advice, remember?"

"Yes." Gaunt sensed what was coming. "And?"

"They're still in a nose-dive." Milton tried persuasion. "Look, Jonny, unload—maybe I could still get you a few days bus-fare back."

Taking the telephone on its cord over to the window, Gaunt looked out at the lakeside view and chewed his lip. Sell now and he'd be losing money he already didn't have. Hold on, and he still had some kind of gamble going.

"No," he said. "They'll rise."

"Like lead balloons," sighed Milton. "Now you want to hear about the girl, right?"

"Right." Gaunt tightened his grip on the receiver, waiting.

"She works for Garrison Properties and they think she's wonderful," said Milton. "Been with them a year, and she's a widow like she told you. Garrison are legitimate as they come—and that little lot's going to cost you a drink if you ever have money again."

"I'll make it a bottle." Gaunt drew a breath of relief. "What about this holiday trip she's on?"

"It was a short-notice thing." Milton sounded slightly puzzled. "But she had time off due and they reckoned she'd been overworking, so they said fine. Jonny, about these shares—"

"No," said Gaunt firmly. "That's final—but thanks."

He hung up, got his driving licence from his wallet, and took out the little scrap of paper with the two Montreux contact names, each with a telephone number. Fanton or Duffrey—neither meant anything to him. Shrugging, he picked up the phone again and dialled Fanton's number.

The line rang out for almost a minute before a male voice answered.

"M'sieu Fanton?" His query only drew a grunt, and he went on cautiously. "A friend suggested I call you as soon as I got in."

"*Attendez* . . . wait," said the voice briefly. There was a pause, then the man came back on the line. "Your friend's name?"

"Falconer."

"I see." The voice became friendly, but still cautious. "He has a secretary. Do you know her given name?"

"Hannah—and he also has a wife," said Gaunt patiently. "If you know him, he still plays a lousy game of golf."

A satisfied chuckle came over the line. "Good, M'sieu Gaunt. Where are you now?"

"At the Hotel Julien." Gaunt found and lit a cigarette one-handed. "There was a telegram waiting."

"*Oui.*" He heard Fanton sigh. "All right, M'sieu Gaunt. Give me ten minutes, then leave the hotel. Drive east along the lakeside maybe three kilometres and there's a cog railway, a little local affair. Take it up and enjoy the view. I'll see you there."

The line went dead and he replaced the receiver.

Gaunt used the ten minutes to unpack and change into clean slacks and a sports shirt. As an afterthought, he slung a camera over one shoulder then turned to leave—at the same moment as there was a knock on the door.

Cursing under his breath, he opened it and Anna Hart smiled in at him. She was in a sleeveless cotton robe, her long dark hair glistening wet, and she was carrying a towel.

"I heard you'd got here, Jonny. You're last of the bunch." She looked past him at the window and the view. "Yes, we're the same—I'm one floor down. There's a roof-top pool too and that's why I look half-drowned." She paused. "Well, do I get to come in?"

"I'm just leaving." He saw her smile begin to fade and added quickly, "Look, I've got to get to a bank and do a couple of things like that. But as soon as I get back—"

"Don't hurry. Not on my account." Her eyes showed a veiled hurt.

"Like hell I won't." Gaunt looked down at her and sighed. "I said as soon as I got back and I meant it—right?"

She nodded with a pretense at meekness then looked down at her bare feet and scratched one against the other like a penitent schoolgirl.

"What's the problem now?" asked Gaunt, coming out into the corridor and closing his door.

"The Walker woman reckons a man of your age on his own is probably bent," she said demurely. "Do I tell her?"

He laughed, put an arm round her waist, and went along with her to the elevator.

Anna got out one floor down. Gaunt stayed aboard until he reached the underground garage then started to walk through the cool, concrete gloom and its rank of cars towards his own.

Then he spotted the powder-pink Triumph, hesitated, looked around, saw no-one, and went over to it. Sliding into the driver's seat, he ran his hand deep beneath the dashboard and felt among the tangle of wiring.

There was nothing there. The gun had gone. Which could mean anything, good, bad, or indifferent.

Scowling, he left the Triumph, got aboard his own car, and drove it out in a way that made the tyres squeal.

CHAPTER 5

The lakeside road out of town was busy but a three-minute drive was still enough to bring Gaunt to the cog-railway station and by then he had forced himself back into a coldly practical mood. He parked the Chrysler in the little station's yard, looked up at the narrow track which climbed a steep thickly wooded hill to another small station just available at the top, then went in and bought a ticket at the tiny booking stall.

The railcar waiting at the platform had a few passengers already aboard. He joined them, took a seat near the top end, and waited patiently while another handful of passengers arrived. At last a uniformed driver ambled over, shooing a pair of latecomers ahead of him. The two, a middle aged man and woman, plumped down in seats in the row below Gaunt, then an engine began to whine and in another moment the railcar was clacking its way up the hill.

Almost immediately they were among the trees and the lake was lost from sight. Clacking on, the railcar passed a matching downward car at the halfway mark and finally sighed to a stop at the top station.

Gaunt got out, emerged in a sunlit concrete yard, and let the other passengers stream past him. The hilltop was occupied by a scatter of small hotels and cafés, but none of the people strolling round seemed interested in his arrival.

Shrugging, he went over to the rail at the edge of the yard, leaned on it, and lit a cigarette while the sun baked against his back.

The view was a tourist spectacular, out across the blue of the lake and its fringe of wooded hillsides, the white, pillar-supported ribbon of a busy autoroute far below and a dark, fang-like line of mountains like a barrier blocking the horizon. Down at the lakeside a steamer was nosing into a pier beside an old castle while a handful of flea-sized sailboats scattered clear.

"If the mountains interest you, they are called the Dents du Midi," said a dry voice.

The middle aged man who had been last to board the railcar came forward and leaned against the rail beside him. He was plump, wore a grey lightweight summer suit with an open-necked white shirt, and was almost totally bald. His leathery face shaped a slight smile as he glanced at Gaunt.

"Willi Fanton," he introduced himself casually, staying against the rail and considering the view. "You see that long brown stain over there, coming from the shore out into the lake? The river Rhone, M'sieu Gaunt—it brings mud down from the mountains, flows in there, then leaves the lake again at Geneva. And from there it travels all the way to the Mediterranean. It is a thought, eh?" He paused, then added softly, "The view is a bonus. Bringing you up here, we could make sure you weren't followed."

"We?" Gaunt looked round and understood. The woman who had boarded the railcar with Fanton was a few paces away.

"Madame Duffrey, your other contact," said Fanton, then saw Gaunt's face. "You didn't expect a woman?"

"I've nothing against them," Gaunt answered wryly.

"*Bon.*" Fanton nodded. "Sara Duffrey is a business-woman, an investment counsellor. Her help could be important to you."

Gaunt looked at the woman with a new interest. Sara Duffrey was a smart, moderately buxom blonde, probably in her late forties, with still attractive looks and intelligent eyes. She wore a simple, sleeveless cotton dress and sandals and carried a shoulder-bag.

"Madame Duffrey is a widow," explained Fanton dead-pan. "Carelessly, her husband fell off a mountain some years ago."

They left the rail and went over. Sara Duffrey greeted Gaunt with a smile and a nod, then Fanton led the way to the nearest open-air café, where a high bank of red, thornless roses threw a patch of shade over some of the tables. As they sat down, a waitress came over for their order and Fanton and Sara Duffrey chose cognac. Gaunt settled for a beer, then, as the girl left them, Fanton cleared his throat politely.

"How was your journey, M'sieu Gaunt?" he asked.

"Interesting." Gaunt gave him a stony look. "I got hit on the head, someone took a shot at me, and I saw a car crash. Now I'm here."

Sara Duffrey chuckled. A chunky diamond and ruby ring glinted as she gestured chidingly towards her companion.

"Let him have his drink first, Willi," she suggested. "I think he feels he has earned it." Then she glanced at

Gaunt again, thoughtfully. "Or maybe he has questions of his own to ask first."

"Like finding out a little more about who I'm talking to, for a start," agreed Gaunt politely.

Fanton frowned. "I told you. Madame Duffrey is a respected investment counsellor—"

Sara Duffrey cut him short with a laugh. "*Mon Dieu,* Willi, don't be so pompous. That, sitting beside you, M'sieu Gaunt, is my brother." She leaned nearer, showing a plump, firm valley of cleavage. "He has a government job, like you, but in the Swiss civil service—and we have both known your Henry Falconer in Edinburgh for a long time, as a friend."

The girl returning with their drinks stopped her there. Fanton paid, then lifted his glass, glanced at his sister, and looked questioningly at Gaunt.

"To Henry Falconer," suggested Gaunt. He sipped his beer, then nodded. "Still want my side of it first?"

They did, and he kept to essentials, trying to stick to fact —and Willi Fanton and his sister proved themselves good listeners, only interrupting with an occasional question, mostly contenting themselves with an understanding nod or an unemotional sip of cognac.

When he finished, Gaunt was conscious it was the first time he'd been able to talk through it all with anyone. The only thing he'd kept back was his indecision over Anna Hart and he stayed stubbornly determined to keep it that way.

"Henry Falconer 'phoned Willi at home last night," said Sara Duffrey quietly. "It was a long call—and the reason why Willi stayed off work today." She paused, her sharp

eyes considering him again. "Henry said you were reliable—
particularly when there was trouble around. *Oui*, I think he
is right. But—" She stopped there and glanced at her
brother.

Willi Fanton nodded slowly. "The news we have for you
just strengthens some of the things you have learned,
M'sieu Gaunt. Henry Falconer's call, for instance—part of
it was to warn you about these men Hubbard and Dawson.
Your police believe they know them, but under other
names."

"And their real background?" asked Gaunt softly.

"A record of violence," said Fanton and shrugged. "So
your theory that they are a hired escort and that the currency is in another of the Safari cars makes sense. Your
candidates for that are still this man Walker and his
wife?"

Gaunt nodded.

"Next"—Fanton frowned and swirled the cognac in his
glass for a moment—"*oui*, it is only gossip, but from a good
source. There is a story that a second consignment of
money was hi-jacked not long ago, but this time on the
French side of the border. The same way as before—the
courier killed and everything left looking like another road
accident."

"Does it check out?" asked Gaunt harshly.

"France is another country," said Fanton carefully. "One
has to be diplomatic about such things. I am trying." He
shaped an encouraging smile. "But there are other things
we can do now. This man in the ambulance, Carl Phillipe,
may be known."

"And Henry Boisson?"

"My department," said Sara Duffrey briskly. She took a slim silver cigar case from her bag, put a small, narrow cheroot between her lips, lit it with a matching silver lighter, and nodded confidently. "Boisson moves round the investment world. I've heard of him, and I can find out more."

"Without upsetting your resident financial gnomes?" queried Gaunt bitterly.

"*Doucement.*" She laid a sympathetic hand on his arm and the diamond and ruby ring sparkled more than ever. "I know—most people think we Swiss don't go to a church to pray, that we go to a bank." She smiled and shook her head. "All right, money pours in from many places. But what our banking system offers is privacy, not secrecy."

"There's a difference?" Gaunt didn't hide his sarcasm.

"In a case like this, when people have been killed, people left dying"—for a moment, there was anger in her eyes—"yes, there are ways." The anger vanished and she smiled again. "There are times, M'sieu Gaunt, when a woman in business has certain advantages over the average male."

Willi Fanton cleared his throat and glanced at his watch. His sister nodded.

"Maybe you would like to leave us," she suggested. "Willi and I will stay a little longer and talk about what we have to do. I promise, you will hear from us soon.

It was more than a hint. Gaunt finished his beer and left them. There was a railcar waiting at the station and it took him clacking back down to the lakeside, where his car lay baking under the sun.

Once behind the wheel, he got out the Montreux street map provided by Safari Suisse and checked where Automo-

biles Tamboure was located. Then he tucked the map away
and glanced up at the hill. Sara Duffrey and her brother
were capable allies—though he wondered how many other
old friends like the buxom blonde were tucked away in
Henry Falconer's contact list, or what Falconer's wife
would do if she ever found out.

But the garage was one firm lead he could take a look at
on his own. The whole cauldron was beginning to bubble.
He didn't feel like letting other people do all the stirring.

It meant a journey almost to the other side of town, past
the souvenir shops and the main bus station, then along an
avenue of tourist hotels which were bright with sun um-
brellas and had gardens which were a blaze of flowers.
Then Gaunt turned off, into a quieter side street of apartment houses and small work yards. From there another
narrow street ended in a T junction with a garage building
at the head of the T.

He pulled in at the kerb some distance away, behind an
old pick-up truck, got out, walked nearer, then stopped and
made a pretence of being interested in a hardware store's
window.

It was a good viewpoint. Automobiles Tamboure was
straight ahead, a single-storey brick building fronted by a
filling station and an *auto-lavage* wash bay. Henry Boisson's black B.M.W. was parked in the forecourt—and the
car just emerging from the car wash was Hubbard and
Dawson's blue Saab. A mechanic drove the car clear, then
left it, the bodywork glinting wet and clean.

Gaunt thought sadly of his own dirt- and insect-smeared
Chrysler, then saw something else which made him slip

quickly into the shelter of the hardware store's doorway. A battered-looking Volkswagen was lying a stone's throw away from him, on the opposite kerb, and the sallow-faced man lounging at the wheel was smoking a cigarette. He wore a grimy tee-shirt—but the last time Gaunt had seen him he'd been driving the Citroen ambulance.

"*Pardon*, m'sieu," said an impatient voice behind him.

Muttering an apology, he eased back to let a customer come out of the shop and kept watching. The Volkswagen's occupant smoked on, with the patience of a man used to waiting—and all his attention was on the Tamboure garage.

Gaunt returned to the Chrysler, got in, and gave a wry grin at his own freckled, sun-reddened reflection in the driving mirror. Hubbard and Dawson had already collected one tail. It wouldn't do any harm to join the party.

He waited a full quarter of an hour. The pick-up truck drove away and a delivery van slipped into its place. Then suddenly, catching Gaunt off guard, the Volkswagen engine started up. A moment later the blue Saab emerged from the garage, turned right into the 'I' junction, and drove off.

The Volkswagen pulled out, following, and Gaunt gave it till it reached the junction and had turned before he began moving.

The driver ahead was keeping a long-distance tail on the blue Saab and Gaunt did the same with him. It meant he only saw the Saab occasionally, when the traffic flow was halted at a crossing. But the route was back in towards the centre of Montreux, though keeping away from the lakeshore.

They passed the railway station and post office, went along another street where every other building seemed to be a bank, then a few moments later the Hotel Julien showed ahead. The Saab's indicator lights signalled and it turned down into the basement car park. Slowing briefly, as if making up his mind, the Volkswagen driver accelerated again and kept straight on past the hotel.

Gaunt stayed with him. The man steered back onto the lakeside road, then headed east, driving impatiently, using his horn when the traffic delayed him.

They passed the foot of the cog railway and still the Volkswagen pressed on—until the tree-fringed grounds of the mediaeval castle by the shore appeared ahead and a lumbering tourist coach unexpectedly jammed its length across the road, trying to swing into the castle's busy parking lot.

The Volkswagen skidded to a halt and the Chrysler was fourth in the queue of cars that halted behind it while the coach driver struggled to complete his turn. There were ice-cream stands and a souvenir stall under the shadow of the turreted, red-roofed old stronghold—but he had no time to see more as the coach lurched in, the road cleared, and the Volkswagen snarled away again.

A few more kilometres went by and the lakeside scenes changed. Small, sandy coves were filled with moored dinghies and small sailboats. The roadside snack bars had nautical names and décor, and only the jagged peaks of the Dents du Midi in the distance brought the reality of geography back into focus.

Suddenly, the Volkswagen swung off the road, bounced along a rough stretch of track, drove through an open gate in a high, white-painted board fence, and vanished from sight. Driving past, Gaunt had a glimpse of a small boat-yard and the Volkswagen stopping outside an office hut.

Another of the roadside snack bars was on ahead. He pulled in when he reached it, tucked the Chrysler out of sight at a parking lot in the rear, and tried to decide what to do next. The board fence ran in an unbroken line around the boatyard area and all he could now see was a tip of a mast and the top ridge of the office hut.

Then the answer came to him with a total, slightly awkward simplicity. The snack bar backed on the lakeshore and a few families of holiday-makers were picnicking close to the water's edge. Some of the hardier were splashing and swimming in the lake.

He stripped down to his underpants, left the car, and walked down towards the strip of sandy beach. No-one paid attention and he reached the water's edge, gritted his teeth at the icy chill as he waded in, then started to swim.

The lake shelved sharply and had unexpectedly strong, eddying currents. He had company, too, in the shape of hundreds of tiny semi-transparent fish no longer than the length of his thumbnail. Swimming out for a spell, using a slow, lazy breast-stroke, Gaunt at last went over on his back and let himself drift until he was opposite the boat-yard.

It had a single slipway, which was empty. A small yacht, the only boat in the yard, lay beached near a couple of large open sheds and the white Citroen ambulance was in-side one of the sheds.

Drifting nearer, Gaunt steadied himself against one of

the boatyard mooring buoys. In a moment a door was flung open at the office hut. A man with one arm in a bandage sling came out, shouted angrily, and waved his good fist in Gaunt's direction.

Waving lazily, Gaunt shoved away from the buoy and swam back the way he had come. Two out of three was good enough. The man who called himself Carl Phillipe couldn't be far away.

Once again, no-one paid any attention as he waded ashore and shivered his way back to the Chrysler. He dried himself off as best he could, dressed, and was humming a tune as he set the car moving again, in towards Montreux.

As journeys went, this one had paid off.

Anna Hart had gone out. There was another of her notes under his room door when he got back to the Hotel Julien.

"FOUND A HAIRDRESSER, BACK LATER." was all it said, and Gaunt remembered it had been that way with Patty too. Whenever her morale had dropped low, she'd vanished somewhere and had her hair done.

But it left him free. When he used the 'phone and tried to call Willi Fanton, there was no reply. He tried Sara Duffrey's number and found himself speaking to her secretary, who could only tell him Madame Duffrey was out for the rest of the day.

He hung up, left his room, and took the elevator down to the hotel lobby. The lobby had a stock exchange teleprint machine in one corner and he glanced at some of the prices. The Zurich exchange was up, the American Dow-Jones index had slid a few points, and the London

F.T. index was in its usual gloomy state. He decided Switzerland wouldn't even have heard of Rhuvalla Construction, turned away, and ambled into the coffee bar.

Which was a mistake. Mrs. Elsie MacLean was there, on her own, perched like a small, cheerful grey mouse on one of the bar stools—and there was no escape.

"Where's your Miss Stewart?" asked Gaunt, paying for a mug of coffee and joining her.

"In bed, out to the world." Mrs. MacLean's face wrinkled with an amused disapproval. "Champagne cocktails this time—I warned her. Two left me feeling dizzy, but she's a silly old fool." She sighed. "You know the trouble, Mr. Gaunt? We're not used to strong drink, either of us."

"You'll just have to keep working on it," agreed Gaunt sympathetically.

She chuckled. "Well, at least she'll have a chance to recover tonight. We're baby-sitting for the Corrans—and if two retired schoolteachers can't cope with one four-year-old bairn there's something far wong. Even if Norah Stewart does have a hangover."

"Tie and gag him first," advised Gaunt. "They're from Glasgow." He drank some of his coffee, then asked, "Where are the Corrans going?"

"Some *son et lumière* show that's on at Chillon Castle." Mrs. MacLean sampled one of the sugar lumps from the bowl in front of her and sucked it delicately. "We'll go some other night."

"Chillon?" Gaunt remembered the castle by the lakeside.

"Didn't you learn poetry at school? 'The damp vault's dayless gloom?' Lord Byron?" Mrs. MacLean heaved a

sigh at his lack of response. "I suppose you were fed a staple diet of Rabbie Burns, poor soul. You—not Burns." She sniffed. "He was just a sex-mad ploughman with an easy tongue. You really don't know?"

Gaunt shook his head.

"That man Byron maybe wasn't much better morally, but he did come here and write *Prisoner of Chillon*," said Mrs. MacLean grimly. "Read it sometime, Mr. Gaunt. It's the lament of a sad creature who spent six years in a dungeon in that place, chained to a pillar." Then her eyes twinkled. "Mind you, I suppose they hosed the place out for him now and again."

Gaunt nodded hastily. "Who else is going on this trip?"

"A few folk." She frowned for a moment and helped herself to another sugar lump. "The Walkers, and I think Mr. Hubbard and his friend. Why don't you go too, and take Anna Hart along? The girl worries me, being on her own."

Mrs. MacLean was considering the sugar lumps again as he left.

With time on his hands, Gaunt told the reception desk he'd be at the Julien's rooftop swimming pool, then took the elevator up. The pool was busy but it had a bar where he didn't know anyone, and he spent the next half hour nursing a glass of beer, admiring the passing bikini parade, and trying to decide how many of the suntans around were natural and how many came out of a bottle of instant bronze.

It was still as hot. The muggy air, scented by the bougainvillaea which climbed from concrete tubs around the bar, seemed more oppressive than ever, and he had a suspicion about the edge of heavy black cloud starting to build over the mountains in the distance.

He finished his beer and thought about another. But the rooftop ended as a sanctuary when he saw Mary Walker arrive. She wore a shiny black one-piece swim-suit which made her look like an overweight whale and her husband was trailing behind carrying an armful of towels. Gaunt quickly eased his way round to the elevator and caught it down to the lobby again.

The reception desk still had nothing for him so he drifted over to have another look at the stock exchange teletype. Two of the Julien's waiters were ahead of him, arguing about the commodity market, but once they'd gone he made a half-hearted effort to read his way through the latest print-out.

Sara Duffrey walked into the lobby a moment later, saw him, and came straight over with an amused twinkle in her eyes.

"Studying form, M'sieu Gaunt?" she asked dryly. "I can tell you it all in a nutshell. The weather is too warm for work, so the local markets are sagging. Tomorrow, if it is cooler, industrials and the banks will do well—but I wouldn't touch insurance."

"Right now I can't touch anything. Not if I want to eat." Gaunt offered her a cigarette. Instead, she took out one of her small black cheroots and accepted a light.

"*Merci.*" She smiled up at him. "I checked with my office and heard you had tried to call me. So I came round, on the chance it was important."

"It could be." Quietly, Gaunt told her about the boat-yard trip and her lips puckered with interest.

"Willi's department," she said calmly. "I'll tell him. Is there more?"

He shook his head.

"*Bon.*" Sara Duffrey flicked cheroot ash on the carpet and scattered it with a deft sideways movement of her shoe. "I have some gossip about Henry Boisson for you, from a usually reliable powder room—like I told you, being a woman sometimes helps." She paused, frowned at him, then asked, "Are you married?"

"I was," said Gaunt neutrally. "Stick with Boisson. I'll keep."

She laughed. "Curiosity—I was certain you had been. Henry Boisson is divorced, and his weakness is that he has a lady friend. But it seems the lady is not completely devoted to M'sieu Boisson, certainly not as much as he believes. Which offers a possibility, *n'est-ce pas?*"

"Where there's a woman, there's a problem," Gaunt admitted. "I've noticed."

"And there's no bitchiness in a monastery?" She took a small, leather-bound notebook from her shoulder-bag, glanced at a page, then looked up, her manner becoming crisply professional. "The rest is fact. Henry Boisson is known in the Geneva and Zurich markets as the apparent front man for a very active investment group. That includes handling large sums of foreign currency—mostly through a fairly complicated set of accounts with Banque Suisse and Crédit Suisse. Lately—"

"Large sums. How large?" interrupted Gaunt.

"Usually a million francs minimum. Say two hundred thousand British pounds, give or take the exchange rate." She paused. "Can I go on?"

"You'd better," he said grimly.

"Lately, it appears he has had troubles. Investment stock has been sold, money has been juggled between accounts." She returned the notebook to her shoulder-bag. "In short, there is a feeling that your M'sieu Boisson is having—ah—cash-flow problems."

"Like having lost two shipments of sterling already." If that was true and Boisson was still in business, Gaunt wondered just how many shipments of hot money for laundering must flow through the man's operation. "How about the girl friend? That could be how word of the shipments leaks out."

"Even your anonymous letter?" Sara Duffrey caught a glimpse of herself in one of the hotel mirrors, frowned, and smoothed a strand of her blonde hair back in place. "Learning more about her shouldn't be too difficult. Ah—where will you be tonight? By then, Willi should have the information you want about the boatyard."

"Maybe at Chillon Castle. The Walkers are going."

"Chillon?" She shrugged. "It's an interesting old place, *formidable* if you're a tourist. But be ready for rain or worse. There's a thunderstorm forecast for tonight."

Gaunt stopped her as she turned to leave.

"Madame Duffrey—"

"Sara," she corrected. "Don't make me feel older than I am."

"Sara, I'd like a favour. Could you check a British share price for me? Rhuvalla Construction—I'd like to know how it opens tomorrow."

"Easily," she agreed, then her attention strayed past him. "Someone else seems to want to talk to you."

He glanced round. Anna was standing near the reception desk watching them.

"I always know when to leave," murmured Sara Duffrey, with a wink. She went away, heading out of the hotel and giving Anna a slight smile and a nod as she passed.

"Someone you know?" asked Anna dryly as Gaunt joined her.

"A friend of a friend—he asked her to look me up," answered Gaunt vaguely, saw the slightly querulous expression on her face, and grinned. "When I start picking up stray women, I'll let you know. Now, do I get to buy you a drink and talk about what we could maybe do tonight?"

"Tonight?" She hesitated. "I'm not sure, Jonny—"

"There's some sort of show on at an old castle," he explained. "It'll mean hiding from the Walkers—they're going, and the Corrans have arranged baby-sitters. But—"

"All right." Her manner changed. "Why not? As long as we eat first. I can't take history on an empty stomach."

The Hotel Julien's dining room had a bustling waiter service, mock crystal chandeliers, and a set menu for package tourists. By seven-thirty it was already busy and it cost Gaunt a ten-franc tip to get a table with a view across the lake. But the waiter who steered them through the crowded restaurant treated Anna royally as a result, then nodded solemnly at Gaunt's choice of a bottle of Johannisberger wine.

"A Swiss wine, m'sieu, from the Valais," he said approvingly, then gave Anna a sly, sideways glance as he filled her glass. "The lady will enjoy it."

"The lady just saw what it costs," muttered Anna as the men went off. "Jonny, are you out of your mind?"

"First-night madness." Gaunt hoped the Rembrancer's expense sheet wouldn't singe at the entry. It was hot in the room, the evening shaping even more oppressively than the afternoon had been, and the collar and tie he was wearing felt tight. He grinned at Anna. "Tomorrow I'll repent."

Tomorrow a whole lot might be happening. As they started their meal, he watched the dark-haired girl almost wistfully. She was in a lightweight grey trouser suit with a simple white shirt-blouse and her only jewellery was a tiny antique gold pendant on a thin, matching choker chain. Her mood for the evening seemed natural enough and lively. But a couple of times he'd caught her off guard and seen something else, indefinable, uncertain, yet far from happy.

Tomorrow . . . he fought the thought back and Anna looked up and smiled at him, her eyes bright in the chandelier lights.

"Tell me something," she said mildly. "Was that blonde you were with this afternoon really someone's friend?"

"Like I said," he agreed.

She wrinkled her noise. "More like someone's aunt, I thought."

He grinned, glad Sara Duffrey wasn't anywhere near to react to that one.

It wasn't too difficult to time their departure for Chillon to match when the Walkers and the Corrans were also leaving. Gaunt drove quietly, keeping behind the other two

Safari cars, while Anna curled in the passenger seat beside
him, her handbag on her lap.

Montreux was a bright sparkle of coloured lights all
along the shore, a lake steamer on an evening cruise had a
band playing on its floodlit afterdeck, and the moon was
out. But over to the east the mountains had vanished
behind black thickening clouds which were spreading out
by the moment.

There were more coloured lights strung among the trees
when they reached Chillon Castle, left the Chrysler in the
parking lot, and joined the steady flow of people heading
towards the entrance gate. On the way a tiny, feathered bat
fluttered past them like an agitated oversized butterfly
through the still, heavy air and a first low mutter of
thunder came from the east.

The distant thunder continued as they went through
and joined the other spectators already occupying the rows
of plank benches erected on scaffolding in the castle courtyard. Gaunt found places for himself and Anna, then
looked round. The Currans were two rows below, the
Walkers a little to their right—and his mouth shaped a silent whistle as he saw Hubbard and Dawson there too.

But he hadn't time to see more. The lights blacked out,
to be replaced after a moment by a single spotlight
focussed on a banner hanging limply from one of the castle
turrets. The *son et lumière* began, against the continued
muted rumble of the faraway storm.

Anna close beside him, Gaunt gave up and settled back
while the floodlight effects began to play round the towers
and turrets of the lakeside stronghold. Aided occasionally

by the appearance of a few figures in mediaeval costumes, the story of how the old Dukes of Savoy had used its thirteenth-century dungeons to hold a series of freedom-seeking Swiss leaders boomed out over the loudspeakers in English, French, and German.

By the time Byron's lament led up to the finale there was a new, outside attraction which had the audience murmuring. Occasional jagged flashes of sheet lightning were silhouetting the distant mountains in awesome style.

The performance ended, the main lights came on, and most of the audience began a prudent, drifting exit towards their cars. Gaunt stalled for time, ready to take his cue from the Walkers, saw them head towards one of the castle archways, where a guide was forming a party, and nudged Anna.

"Let's do the whole bit while we're here," he suggested easily.

She nodded, and they threaded their way down the stepped seating. But as they reached the cobbled courtyard Gaunt slowed for an instant, fighting down surprise.

Henry Boisson was at the archway ahead. He was talking earnestly to James Walker while Walker's wife played an uncharacteristic listening role. Walker nodded, the burly, bearded garage owner grinned and slapped him on the shoulder, and they parted.

"We know him, don't we?" said Anna in an odd voice.

Gaunt nodded, pondering the significance of the meeting. "He made that special servicing offer—Automobiles Tamboure."

"I remember." She said it with a frown.

Boisson had walked a few paces to where a tall, blonde girl stood waiting. She was wearing a leather jacket and skirt and had an attractive but sulky-looking face, but smiled as he took her arm. They came straight towards Gaunt and Anna though it wasn't till the last moment that Boisson seemed to spot them.

"*Magnifique* . . . two more of you!" he declared with a beam, and turned to the girl. "Janine, these are more of the Safari people I met at the motel."

The blonde gave Anna a minimal nod, treated Gaunt to a slightly more interested glance, but said nothing.

"You're as big a surprise," said Gaunt dryly. "I didn't think locals would come to a tourist show like this one."

"It was Janine's idea. She wanted a change." Boisson shrugged and squeezed the blonde's arm. "Now, I think maybe she regrets it."

"All I want is to get away before this storm breaks," she said with a grimace. "Henry—"

A nearer flash of lightning, then a deeper rumble of thunder stopped her there and Boisson nodded a quick agreement.

"You both remember my offer?" he asked.

"If it's the way you told it," said Anna. "Half the regular cost."

"Agreed." Boisson smiled at them. "Just don't leave it too long."

He went off with the girl. Gaunt went over with Anna to join the queue of tourists now filing in through the archway and, still wondering, took a quick glance back. Boisson had stopped further along the courtyard, the blonde still at his side, and was talking to another man who seemed vaguely familiar. Then the queue moved forward again, and he had to follow.

Their guide for the Chillon tour was a fair-haired young Swiss student who talked in a clipped, flat monotone and used a pocket comb every couple of minutes. There were about thirty in the party that began wending its way through the dimly lit labyrinth of stairs and corridors, pausing every now and again while he described some feature. Frank and Maggie Corran were up near the front of the group, with the Walkers not far behind—and as the guide led them on, through a large banquet hall hung with flags and armour, Gaunt heard his name called lazily.

"Thought I saw you outside," said Tom Hubbard. The balding, bulky Englishman was leaning against a massive stone fireplace, hands in his pockets and his face a near scowl. He jerked his head to where Dawson was peering up at an old crossbow. "I'll bet he'd like one of these to play with."

"And an apple?" suggested Gaunt.

Hubbard blinked, the inference lost, then he grinned at Anna.

"Why don't we ditch these two and find ourselves somewhere better?" he suggested acidly.

She gave him a frostily polite smile. Winking at Gaunt, he moved on.

The thunderstorm was still creeping its way across towards them. As the young Swiss guide invited them to look through the window slits at the water lapping the stonework and rock below, more brilliant flashes seared between the sky and the lake's surface and one loud peal of thunder seemed to shake the old stone walls.

"Most useful, such a location," said the guide earnestly, combing his hair again. "For defence, for sanitation, for everyting, *oui?* And now *les cachots* . . . the dungeons, okay?"

They went down a narrow, winding staircase into what could have been an old, damp basement lit by bare electric light bulbs. The guide seemed to like this part of his tour.

"Up there"—he pointed to a worn wooden beam—"the gallows. These pillars still have the marks of chains. The rack and the torture irons—all these and more were in daily use." He stopped with some pride at a large, floor-level hole in the wall with a protective barrier rail round it and a glint of lake water outside. "When a prisoner died, he went straight out here—good-bye. What the ladies would call waste disposal, eh?"

He got one or two half-hearted, slightly nervous laughs as the thunder slammed again. On this kind of night, Chillon's atmosphere was too real and brooding for jokes or amusement. Disappointed, he beckoned the group on again and up another flight of stairs to a series of small, partially furnished rooms and one-time defence points.

The party split as they explored. Gaunt was last in a small queue squeezing in through yet another doorway when something round and hard and all too familiar rammed against the base of his spine.

"*Doucement* . . . no fuss," said a cold murmur in his ear. "We back out, slowly. Understand?"

Anna was just one of half a dozen people almost within

touching distance ahead. But he obeyed, tight-lipped, while the gun in his back kept its steady pressure and he was prodded down the corridor again and round a corner into a larger, empty area.

"Stop," he was ordered. "Against the wall."

The gun stayed against his back as he obeyed. A hand frisked him quickly, then there was a grunt and the gun was removed.

Gaunt turned from the wall while the thunder rumbled on outside. The man facing him was thin and dark-haired, with sunken eyes which were totally devoid of expression. He wore a black nylon windcheater jacket, and the automatic pistol in his right hand, a silenced Mauser, was trained unwaveringly on Gaunt's middle.

It was the man he'd seen Boisson talking to earlier. Another memory flooded back. Before that, he'd been working at the car wash outside Boisson's garage.

"We are going to walk together, straight out of here, m'sieu," said the man in the same soft, matter-of-fact voice. "Then to the car park." The gun twitched a warning. "One stupid move, one word—"

"And afterwards?" asked Gaunt bitterly.

The man gave a faint, disinterested shrug which carried its own chill message.

"Here or outside," he said indifferently, while the muzzle of the Mauser shifted, to line up with Gaunt's stomach. "Here I would make slower—and a lot more painful."

Dry-lipped, Gaunt tried to gauge his chances of getting at the gun, of making any kind of break, and knew they were non-existent where he stood.

"*Maintenant,*" said the gunman curtly. "Move."

But suddenly his pale cold eyes widened in sheer disbelief—and a single shot rang out, the sharp report blending with a new rumble of thunder. Frozen by sheer disbelief, Gaunt watched him stagger back against the wall, dropping the gun and clutching his chest with both hands.

Then, face contorted, he lurched away from it again and moved in a drunken, weaving slow-motion which took him staggering out of sight out the doorway at the other end.

"Oh God," said Anna Hart in a hoarse whisper. "Jonny—"

She was standing a few feet away, face drained of colour, gradually lowering the automatic pistol she still gripped in both hands. When Gaunt reached her, she was trembling.

"Easy," he soothed, still hardly believing what had happened. "It's all right."

"I couldn't find you. I"—she swallowed hard—"I came looking—"

He nodded his understanding. No-one else seemed to have heard the shot. It would have been more of a miracle if they had, with the thunderstorm almost overhead.

"Wait here," he said grimly. "Don't move. Right?"

She leaned against the wall, nodding. Scooping up the Mauser the man had dropped, Gaunt went out through the doorway. He paused at the top of a short, winding stairway, took a first few steps down, then stopped again and slowly tucked the Mauser in the waistband of his slacks.

Boisson's man was lying on his back at the foot of the steps, sightless eyes staring up at the bare electric bulb above.

He went down, saw the spreading stain of blood on the man's shirt front and the bullet-hole in his chest, then bent over him and grimly searched his pockets. He found a worn leather wallet, pocketed it, then looked around thoughtfully.

He was on the dungeon level. Through another archway he could see the old wooden gallows beam. Taking a deep breath, Gaunt stooped and heaved the dead man over one shoulder. Then, grunting under the weight, he carried his burden along to the hole in the outer wall that the Chillon garrison of long ago had used so often for the same purpose he had in mind.

Grimacing, he got the limp body over the barrier rail and gave it a final heave. The dead man fell through the hole, there was a splash, and a new flash of lightning seconds later showed the half-submerged corpse floating free, the lake's currents already beginning to drag it away.

Feeling strangely tired, Gaunt went back up to where Anna was waiting. She hadn't moved and stared at him without speaking.

"He got away," he lied, saw the instant relief in her eyes, and nodded at her gun. "No sense in trying to look for him —he couldn't have been badly hurt and made it. So tuck that damned thing away and let's get out of here."

Silently, she put the Browning automatic in her handbag, closed it, and moved without protest when he took her arm.

The rest of the tour group had left the castle and a first few heavy drops of rain were beginning to fall as they reached the exit archway. The fair-haired guide gave a brief smile and a nod as they went past, and Gaunt steered a direct course for the almost deserted car park.

They reached the Chrysler just as the full fury of the rainstorm broke overhead in a deafening clap of thunder. Gaunt got Anna in on the passenger side, tumbled into his own seat a moment later, slammed the door, then sat back while the drumming downpour hammered on the metal roof.

"Anna." He waited till she faced him. "We're going to drive out of here. Then we're going to stop and talk. Talk about you, that gun—all of it."

She nodded dumbly and he started the engine.

CHAPTER 6

The battering downpour formed a glittering white curtain in the Chrysler's lights as Jonathan Gaunt drove away from Chillon and the lakeside. He took a valley road without caring where it led, splashed the car through flooded dips, and only rarely glanced at his passenger. Anna Hart's face was a mere silhouette in the dashboard lighting, her hands were clenched in her lap, and she winced at the occasional scaring flash and blast overhead—but she said nothing.

A closed level crossing came up. Gaunt stopped near the lowered barrier pole, waiting while the crossing's warning bell kept up its slow, monotonous clang, and after a moment a brightly lit passenger train rumbled past. The passengers in the brown and grey carriages, totally insulated in comfort from the storm, were suddenly people he envied.

But the train also acted like an anchor to reality. Once the barrier lifted, Gaunt drove a little way on, then drew the car in at the verge and switched off the engine and lights.

"You wanted to talk," said Anna in a low voice before he could begin. "Jonny, tell me one thing first—please. I—well, I asked before once. Why did you come to Switzerland?"

"To do a job." He sat back and waited, his face expressionless, watching the torrent of water pouring down the windscreen. "To try to plug a leak in the Exchange Control regulations."

"Because of a letter?" She gripped his arm, and added, "It was posted in Geneva, Jonny. Do you want me to tell you what it said?"

He stared at her, not totally taken by surprise but still startled by the vehemence in her voice.

"You?" he asked. "You wrote it?"

She nodded.

"Why?"

"I had reasons—good reasons." She fumbled in her handbag for her cigarettes, lit one, and the tip glowed bright red as she drew on the smoke. "I've a sister, Jonny—you never met her, but she's a couple of years younger than I am. She has a year-old baby, a girl, called Anna after me." She drew quickly, angrily, on the cigarette again. "Her husband was a feckless, likeable fool—and a crook."

"Was?" Gaunt frowned at her, puzzled but beginning to understand.

She nodded. "He's dead. His name was Bill Anderson. What my sister didn't tell me till afterwards was that he'd lost his last straight job months before and had got involved in a currency smuggling ring—they used him as a courier."

"Driving on the Montreux run." He finished it for her and pursed his lips. "Who was he working for?"

"He didn't tell her and said he was being well paid to keep his mouth shut. But he made three trips, then told her there had been problems and things were being changed. He'd need to make just one more trip, then they'd use him only at the British end." She paused, a new bitterness in her voice. "He made a joke about what they were going to do—how they'd use ordinary tourists on the Safari Suisse package trips to Montreux and it would be totally foolproof, no risks."

A new lightning flash seared through the rain. For a moment the pitiless light showed her face tight and angry, then it was a mere silhouette in the darkness again.

"There was a rumour," said Gaunt quietly. "One I only heard today—that a currency consignment was hi-jackcd on the French side of the border. We knew about one before that, when the driver was killed." He rubbed a hand slowly across his chin, so much making sense now. "What happened to Anderson?"

"Officially?" She shrugged at him. "A car crash—on the French side of the border, like you said, when he was on his way out. His car left the road, caught fire, and burned out."

"And your sister?"

"Tried to commit suicide when she got the news," said Anna. "God knows why, but she loved him." Wearily, she mashed her cigarette out on the dashboard. "But, like I told her in the hospital, at least she still has their child. That's more than—well, some people."

"Then what happened?" probed Gaunt, sensing he had to move her on, and quickly.

"She told me what she knew and—well, he'd let slip the date of the first Safari consignment, and that it would be out of Edinburgh." Her fists tightened on her lap again. "I wanted to hit back at those people, whoever they were— but in a way they couldn't trace back to his widow."

"So you wrote a letter." Gaunt swallowed hard, glad that

the darkness hid his own expression. "Postmarked Geneva —how?"

She shrugged in a matter-of-fact way. "I took a day off work, flew out in the morning, posted it, flew home in the afternoon. I thought it would make it more authentic."

"It did," agreed Gaunt dryly. "But after that, why sign up for the same Safari?"

"I wanted to make sure something did happen," she said simply.

"And the gun?" Gaunt saw her hesitate and sighed. "Look, I've known you had it ever since Dover. I worry about women who pack a .38 when they go on holiday— worry enough to wonder what else they've got in mind."

"But you didn't say anything, didn't do anything." She looked at him, smiled a little, and shook her head. "Why?"

"Hell, I don't know," he confessed. "But believe me, I'm glad—now."

Her smile vanished at the reminder. "It belonged to my husband. I'd—well, I'd just kept it with a few other things." She stopped and sighed. "Bringing it seemed sensible, a kind of insurance, but I never really thought about how it would be if I had to use it. Not till tonight."

Gaunt thought of the thin-faced man and those pale, sunken eyes, and fought down a momentary feeling of revulsion at the way he'd dumped his body. Instead, he grinned.

"You're a lousy shot," he said easily. "But if you hadn't come along—"

"He was going to kill you." She made it a statement of fact.

He nodded.

"And now—when he didn't?"

He didn't answer, because he didn't know.

The rain was easing, the thunderstorm had passed, and to the east the jagged peaks of the Dents du Midi were showing again, harsh and yet welcome in the moonlight. He glanced at the dashboard clock, shrugged at the inevitable, and reached for the ignition key.

Anna reached for his hand and stopped him.

"Jonny, I'm sorry," she said simply.

"You damned well should be," he said dourly. Then kissed her.

On the drive back, he told Anna Hart a little of what he knew—a little, because she'd earned that much, but no more, and even that only after extracting a reluctant promise from her not to get involved.

"But you mean you still aren't sure who has the money?" she persisted again as they reached the outskirts of Montreux.

"Let's say it's narrowing down," he temporised, and grinned at her. "There was a time when I thought it might be you."

But, he told himself, the Walkers still looked the soundest bet—except that ever since the Safari had started most things that had looked that way had come unstuck.

Gaunt sighed under his breath as the car purred on through the wet and glistening streets. Even if he ended with a lead which meant a finish to the British end of Boisson's operation, how many more money laundries were operating? Maybe that wasn't his problem. Maybe there were even similar outfits running money illegally out of some countries into Britain—and how righteous was Britain going to be about that kind of help to the balance of payments?

Not for the first time, he decided it was a crazy, mixed-up world.

They reached the Hotel Julien a minute or so later and he drove the Chrysler down into the underground garage—then gave a soft whistle of surprise and glanced quickly at Anna.

A police motorcycle was parked at the far end of the access lane and a policeman in a white crash-helmet was in the centre of a knot of people standing further along, under one of the neon tube lights.

"What's wrong now?" asked Anna in a sharp, worried voice. Then she looked at the group again and added in surprise, "It's the Walkers!"

She was right. Relieved and his interest equally roused, Gaunt backed the Chrysler into a vacant space, checked that the Mauser was securely hidden in his waistband, and locked the car once they'd got out. Then they walked over.

The police motorcyclist was listening with a strained sympathy to a tirade from Mary Walker while two of the hotel porters formed a blandly unconcerned audience. James Walker stood a little to one side and gave them a grim nod as they approached.

"Trouble?" asked Gaunt.

"Our damn car's been stolen," said Walker bitterly. "Vanished out of here"—he snapped finger and thumb together—"just like that."

"What happened?" asked Anna with a startled, sideways glance at Gaunt.

"It's easy enough to tell," grated Walker sourly. "We came back from the castle and had a drink in the bar. Then—well, it was about twenty minutes ago. Mary discovered she'd left her handbag in the car and I got sent down for it." He shrugged. "No car."

"How long had you been away from it?" asked Gaunt, with a sick feeling he'd been out-manoeuvred yet again.

"Half an hour at most." Walker thumbed gloomily at the motorcyclist. "That's the total reaction from the police so far. And all we've got out of the hotel is a few twittering noises."

Gaunt looked at him closely. Walker was angry, but not panic stricken . . . and behind him the policeman turned from Mary Walker, closed his notebook, and shrugged at the hotel porters.

"*Bien, c'est tout,* M'sieu Walker," he said briskly. "A full description of your car will be circulated—believe me, it will turn up."

"When?" asked Walker bleakly.

The policeman shrugged. "When it happens, we will be in touch. Naturally, everyone regrets such a thing should happen."

He touched his crash-helmet, went back to his machine, started it up, and went roaring away.

"It better turn up," said Mary Walker in an agitated voice. Her moon-shaped face quivered with anger. "What are we expected to do? Walk home?"

"We're insured," soothed Walker.

"Great," she snapped.

"And all our luggage was out of it," added Walker in an attempt at consolation. He turned to Anna for more understanding. "We left it locked—"

"Or so you say," snapped his wife. "Her car is still here, everybody else's car is still here. Why take ours?"

Gaunt stayed silent, Anna said nothing, and she switched her wrath to the hotel porters. That gave Gaunt and Anna the chance to say good night to Walker and go over to the elevator.

"Well?" asked Anna quietly as the door closed.

He nodded slowly. "Their car—it could be."

"You mean it has to be," she protested.

"Maybe, maybe not," said Gaunt cryptically. "But the way things are, I'll pass that one to someone else." He reached for the elevator buttons. "I want to check with the reception desk. Stay with me for a drink?"

"I'm tired, Jonny." She shook her head with some reluctance. "Tired and confused. No, I'll go straight up."

He nodded his understanding and set the elevator moving. As it rose, she looked worried.

"Suppose these people try again—" she began.

"One way or another, they've other things to bother about now," he assured her, and hoped he was right.

He left the elevator at the ground floor, then stayed to watch the indicator lights wink their way up and stop at the seventh. He was thinking of Boisson talking to the Walkers at the castle, of the girl who had been with him, of what had happened afterwards—and it was a flip of a coin which of the possibilities left open made the most sense.

There was no message for him at the reception desk. Turning away, he glanced at his watch and saw it was nearly 1 A.M. He felt tired, but he still wanted a drink and headed for the bar.

It was busy. But he stopped short at the door and took a quick half-step backward for another reason. Hubbard and Dawson was there, leaning side by side halfway along the bar counter. Hubbard was laughing at something and Dawson had a grin on his face.

They hadn't spotted him. He moved away, back across the lobby, frowning.

Everything pointed to the two men having ridden shotgun escort all along the journey. But how much else did they know, how much more were they involved? For the moment at least, from the way they were acting, they hadn't a care in the world.

Because the Walkers' car didn't matter, or because they knew who had stolen it? He scowled in a way that made the clerk at the reception desk blink. Did they even know about Boisson's man being sent to kill him and that it had gone wrong?

Giving up, he took the elvator up to his floor, went along to his room, and unlocked the door.

He was still thinking as he stepped into the darkened room. But an instant later, as he reached for the light switch, his nostrils caught the scent of tobacco smoke—and a table light snapped on as he reached for the gun in his waistband.

"*Bon soir*," said Willi Fanton politely, smiling up at him from the room's only armchair. "Did you enjoy your—ah—evening?"

"No." Gaunt relaxed with a sigh, closed the door behind him, then sat on the edge of the bed and glared at Fanton. "How the hell did you get in here?"

"The usual way. I bribed someone. It was necessary—I want to talk to you."

"That goes both ways." Gaunt brought out the Mauser and tossed it on the bed, then placed the dead man's wallet beside it. "How long have you been up here?"

"About an hour." The Swiss looked pensively at the gun and wallet, then raised an eyebrow at Gaunt. "Why?"

"The Walkers' car has been stolen."

Fanton sat bolt upright and winced. "Boisson?"

"You tell me," said Gaunt.

"*Formidable*," murmured Fanton. He thumbed at the bed. "And these?"

"From an unfriendly native at Chillon tonight."

Fanton's thin lips puckered in a silent whistle. "And what happened to this native?"

"With luck, he's on his way to the Mediterranean," said Gaunt cryptically.

"*Pardon?*" Fanton blinked, then understood and gave a slow nod. "The lake—I see." He picked up the wallet, examined its contents for a few moments while his bald head glinted under the table light, then frowned up. "A few francs—nothing else, no identification?"

"No, but he worked at Boisson's garage."

"A pity." Fanton put the wallet in his pocket. "It means Boisson has you marked as some kind of an enemy, maybe even on the hi-jacking side." He shrugged sadly. "It ends your usefulness in that direction, agreed?"

His tone of voice made Gaunt feel he had become a liability. But he said nothing. Fanton considered the Mauser, then shrugged again.

"M'sieu Gaunt, I haven't heard anything you said, I haven't seen anything," he said. "But I will tell you briefly what brought me here. The boatyard you are interested in belongs to Carl Phillipe Renan, whose description seems to match your 'patient' in the ambulance—except that he is totally fit and well."

"Anything else known about him?" asked Gaunt.

"Very little, except that he first appeared in Montreux about a year ago, when he took over the boatyard." Fanton built a slow, thoughtful steeple with his fingertips. "However, Sara has discovered a little more about the lady Boisson is interested in. She is blonde, her name is Janine Davelle, she sometimes works as a night-club singer—and she has been seen a few times with a man who could be your Carl Phillipe."

"She was with Boisson at Chillon," Gaunt told him.

"*Merci.*" It was hard to tell if Fanton was being sarcastic. He studied his fingertips again. "Could she have been your letter-writer?"

Gaunt shook his head. "It was Anna Hart—she told me tonight."

"Your young widow," mused Fanton. "Why?"

"That rumour you heard about the second hi-jack. Her sister's husband was killed in it." Gaunt got up from the bed, went over to the window, and looked at the twinkle of lights down below. "Right now, I'm more interested in the Walkers' car."

He told Fanton what little he knew, and the Swiss scratched his bald head, equally puzzled.

"First Boisson's man tries to kill you, then this—" Fanton paused and swore softly to himself. *"C'est possible* . . . perhaps it was all arranged because he was afraid to wait until tomorrow. But on the other hand—"

"We don't damned well know," said Gaunt.

"But we are likely to find out," prophesied Fanton. He got to his feet, went over to the door, then considered Gaunt again. "One thing is certain. Boisson now knows you are still alive and that will not please him, even if he is uncertain about how much you know. I—ah—would keep your room locked tonight."

He left, closing the door behind him.

Gaunt stayed by the window, lit a cigarette, and stayed there for a spell looking out at the twinkling lights and the moonlit lake without really seeing them.

Then, wearily, he crushed out what was left of the cigarette in an ashtray and decided he might as well get some sleep.

But the Mauser pistol was under his pillow when he at last got between the sheets and he had used the extra security bolt on the door.

He'd never been a Boy Scout, but "Be Prepared" made a good motto.

Morning came with a clear blue sky, bright enough to hurt the eyes. Lake Geneva lay like a calm, unruffled pool, as if there had never been a storm, and several big brown and gold fish hawks were lazily circling overhead, searching for breakfast.

Gaunt had slept like a log. He shaved and dressed,

'phoned down for breakfast, ate it in his room, and by then it was 9 A.M. Checking the Mauser, he found it held a full clip of fat seven-millimetre Parabellum cartridges and after a moment's thought he left the silencer in place. He didn't like silencers. They made any gun clumsy and awkward to handle or conceal. But if he was forced into using the pistol, then he had no intention of advertising it.

The Mauser was back in the waistband of his slacks, concealed by a loose gabardine sports jacket, when he left his room and took the elevator down to the Hotel Julien lobby. Telling the reception clerk he was going out, he bought a fresh pack of cigarettes from a machine then saw a gloomy-looking James Walker limping in from the street.

"Any news of your car yet?" asked Gaunt.

"Nothing." Walker gave a tired sigh and stuck his hands in his pockets. "Mary sent me round to talk to the local gendarmes—she reckoned we weren't getting anywhere by 'phoning." He scowled. "There's times when that woman imagines she can command miracles. Believe me, after the kind of night I've had about the damned car I wish they'd taken her with it—but I should be so lucky!"

Gaunt made a sympathetic noise, puzzling again whether the man's reactions were genuine.

"One thing I've got to do is 'phone that Tamboure garage place," added Walker in the same disgruntled voice. "We were supposed to take the car along there today—remember the half-price service offer?"

"From Boisson?" Gaunt nodded. "I saw him talking to you at the castle last night."

"Yes. That was what it was about." Walker sighed again

and squared his shoulders. "Well, I'd better go up and break the happy news. Maybe she'll just throw me out a window."

They parted and Gaunt went down to the underground garage. The hotel had a private security man on duty at the exit, a new, overnight public relations touch even if he was just sitting on a stool reading a comic book. Taking the Chrysler out, Gaunt drove it round to the nearest filling station, had the tank topped up, the oil level and tyre pressures checked, and rang Willi Fanton's number from the filling station's pay 'phone.

There was no reply. When he tried Sara Duffrey's number he got the engaged tone and it stayed that way when he waited a couple of minutes and tried again. He cursed and hung up, feeling that maybe Fanton had been right and that his usefulness had pretty well ended—at least as far as his instructions from the Remembrancer's Department went.

He'd been away less than an hour when he took the Chrysler back to the Julien garage, left it there, and noticed that Hubbard and Dawson's blue Saab was no longer in sight.

"*Oui*, they left just after you did, m'sieu," said the security man when Gaunt asked him. He raised an inquisitive eyebrow. "When they come back, should I give them any message?"

Gaunt shook his head and went back up to the lobby. It was busy, a whole coach-load of new arrivals and their luggage being booked in at the desk, and he was skirting round the temporary turmoil when he heard his name called and saw an arm waving in his direction. Another moment and Mrs. MacLean and Miss Stewart had burrowed their way through the activity round and were at his side, smiling at him like two small, eager grey terriers.

"There you are," said Mrs. MacLean almost accusingly. "And where do you think you've been, young man?"

He grinned down at them. "Out—not for long. Why?"

"Well, it's lucky we saw you," said Miss Stewart in a disapproving voice. "Men—they behaved differently when I was your age." Then she wrinkled her nose. "Maybe that was what was wrong."

He nodded patiently. "So what am I supposed to have done?"

"Left that girl Anna Hart searching everywhere for you," said Mrs. MacLean sternly. "Running round and looking worried. Now, it's none of our business, but—"

"I'll find her," he promised with an immediate sense of foreboding. "She's still in the hotel?"

"She said she'd be," agreed Miss Stewart, and glanced at her friend. "Ready, Elsie?"

"Going somewhere?" asked Gaunt.

The two elderly faces beamed and Miss Stewart nodded. "Our waiter told us about a casino in town where they play something called blackjack in the mornings."

"We're going to broaden our education," explained Mrs. MacLean. "Now you go and find that girl."

Gaunt left them, went straight to one of the lobby telephones, and asked for Anna Hart's room. The moment he was connected the receiver at the other end seemed to be scooped up and she was on the line.

"I'm in the lobby," said Gaunt. "Anything wrong."

"Yes." He heard her turn away and speak quickly to

someone in the background, then she was back on the line. "Come up, Jonny. Right now."

Her 'phone went down. Replacing his own receiver, he squeezed into the elevator with a cluster of the new guests and their luggage, tried to keep his patience as they took a long time over getting out at the fourth floor, got out at the seventh, and hurried along to Anna's room. She opened the door at his knock and gravely beckoned him in. As the door closed again, he saw Frank and Maggie Corran were in the room.

"What's happened?" he asked Anna, his heart sinking as he saw the Corrans' expressions.

Frank Corran was standing at the window, his normally cheerful young face white and strained. He had a cigarette cupped in one hand and when he raised it to his lips the hand was shaking. Maggie Corran was in a chair, staring up at Gaunt. There was a total desperation in her manner and her eyes were red from weeping.

"Tell him, Frank," said Anna quietly. "You must."

Swallowing, Corran glanced at his wife in a tortured way and she gave the smallest of nods.

"They've got Peter," he said dully and moistened his lips. "I—well, I reckon you know what they want, don't you?"

Gaunt stared at him, suddenly understanding, a picture of the Corran's four-year-old coming into his mind.

"You mean your car is the one?" he asked.

Maggie Corran gave a speechless nod.

"And these people mean it, whoever the hell they are," said Corran. "We'll get Peter back if they get the car. But then what happens—to all three of us?"

"Anna?" Gaunt turned to her, the obvious, unspoken question on his lips.

"Their room is next door to this." She gave a small shrug. "I went down for breakfast late, then when I came back up—well, their balcony window was open, so was mine. I heard Maggie crying, heard them talking—"

"Then she came through and told us about you," said Corran. "Gaunt, you've got to believe me. They said if we contacted the police or the people we're supposed to deliver to, did anything—"

"They?" asked Gaunt.

"We don't know," said Maggie Corran in a tight, almost hysterical voice. "That makes it even worse. We don't know who they are. Just—just that they've got Peter." She closed her eyes and shook her head. "God, why did we ever get into any of this?"

A siren blast reached them from one of the little white pleasure steamers out on the lake. The sun was pouring into the room, throwing Frank Corran's shadow in sharp relief across the floor.

"And they just told you, like that?" Gaunt asked Anna.

"Let's say the real persuasion was getting them to see you," she said dryly. "But I promised you'd help, that you could help."

"But no police, nothing like that," insisted Corran earnestly. "I—hell, Gaunt. He's our son. I—" He ended it there, helplessly.

"Do you know what you've been carrying in that car?" asked Gaunt deliberately.

Corran shook his head. "No. Except it isn't drugs. I said

I"—he glanced at his wife—"I said we wouldn't carry drugs."

Gaunt sighed, ran a hand along his chin, and mentally congratuled Henry Boisson for his cleverness. Almost everything had been the way he'd thought except that Boisson had deliberately, delicately at first, drawn attention to the Walkers' car. Used it as an innocent decoy bait.

But now the hi-jackers had a different kind of bait for a different purpose. One four-year-old boy . . . whatever way they'd arrived at the truth.

"Let's start with what matters," he said slowly. "Tell me how it happened, everything you can remember."

Corran bit his lip. "We ate breakfast in the restaurant because room service costs more. After that, I went out on my own to buy some camera film." He went to his wife and laid a comforting hand on her shoulder. "You—well, you'll have to ask Maggie the rest."

"Well, Maggie?" asked Gaunt gently.

"There's a children's paddling pool beside the rooftop pool," she said in a low, dull voice. "I took Peter up there and he started splashing around, playing with a couple of other children—" She stopped, her hands clasping and unclasping in her lap, then picked it up again with a visible effort. "He asked for something to drink, so I went over to the pool bar and got him a lemonade. But when I came back with it—" This time, when she stopped, she couldn't go on.

"He was gone," said Frank Corran harshly. "One of the other kids said Peter's daddy had taken him away—any man is a 'daddy' at that age." He shrugged. "But Maggie just thought I had got back and maybe taken him down to the room for some reason."

"You came down?" asked Gaunt.

She nodded.

"And?"

"The 'phone was ringing." Her voice was almost a whisper. "This man just said he had Peter, that nothing would —would happen to him if we were sensible. Then he hung up."

"He called again," said Frank Corran wearily. The cigarette in his hand had burned down almost to his fingers and he stubbed it blindly in an ashtray. "I'd just got back to the room and Maggie had told me."

"How long has he been missing?"

"An hour—no, maybe a little less." Corran made a clumsy job of lighting a fresh cigarette.

"And the second call told you what you were to do?"

"Yes. Then—well, Maggie broke down and Mrs. Hart came into it."

"I brought them through here," said Anna. "In their own room, with Peter's toys everywhere—"

"Look, Gaunt," said Corran hoarsely. "She says you're some kind of government man. Right—we don't care. We don't care about anything now, except getting Peter back. But what do we do?" He gestured despairingly. "If we turn the car over to these people, we get Peter back. But then what happens when the other mob finds out? What will they do to us, all three of us?"

"You'll get protection," promised Gaunt grimly. "But let's concentrate on getting the boy first."

He thought hard as he spoke. Carl Phillipe's hi-jack squad had had all night to discover the Walkers' car was a decoy and to somehow learn the truth. After that, they hadn't wasted time—but having laid their hands on Peter Corran, how had they got him out of the hotel? Suddenly, the answer to that one came to him with an astounding simplicity.

"Let me check something," he told them. "I'll be right back. Anna will stay with you." ·

Two minutes later Gaunt stepped out of the elevator that had taken him down to the Hotel Julien's underground garage. The same security man was still sitting near the exit and gave him a lazy grin of recognition.

"Still looking for your friends, m'sieu?" he asked.

"No, something else this time," said Gaunt easily. "Did you see a man drive out with a small boy? They maybe left about an hour ago."

"*Mais oui,* if you mean the child who was sick," said the man with a sympathetic frown. "They took him away in an ambulance—*un accident,* they said. But he have good doctors here in Montreux."

"Was it a private ambulance, a white Citroen?" asked Gaunt slowly.

The man nodded and that was all he needed to know.

He told the Corrans when he got back up to Anna's room. It didn't make much difference to them, but Anna understood.

"Then that means there's a chance—" she began.

Gaunt stopped her with a quick, warning nod.

"Let's get a few more things sorted out," he told the Corrans. "You knew you were smuggling—smuggling something. How was the contact made originally?"

"A couple of weeks after we made the Safari booking," said Frank Corran. "I run a TV repair shop, right? This character came in, said he knew we were going and that business hadn't been too hot for me—then he offered five hundred pounds if we'd do the job." His mouth tightened. "No risks, he said, and I was fool enough to talk Maggie into agreeing."

"Then?"

"Frank had to give him the car for a weekend," said Maggie Corran, looking up. She'd been crying again, but her voice was steadier and there was a dawning hint of hope in her eyes. "They—whatever they did, it just looked the same when we got it back."

"But we got half the money, the rest to come when we got home," said Corran. He paused. "Look, does it matter right now? I mean—"

"It matters," said Caunt. "What was the delivery arrangement?"

"We'd be told when we got here." Corran gave a humourless laugh. "We were—you saw that character Boisson at the castle last night? Well, he 'phoned us here first. I've to take the car to his Automobiles Tamboure place at noon today, book it in under his half-price service offer, then pick it up tonight—and it's done." His mouth trembled. "Or—or that's the way it was going to be."

"It's 10 A.M. now," said Anna, glancing at her watch. "Jonny, that's just two hours—"

"And what's the other way, Frank?" asked Gaunt in a flat, level voice. "What's the way you've to do it if you want your son back?"

"Drive out of here just before noon." Corran licked his lips nervously. "But head straight for the Chillon Castle parking lot—and leave the car there with the key in the ignition."

"Then?" Anna frowned at them.

"There's a cruise boat which leaves Chillon soon after that," said Maggie Corran tonelessly. "We take the two-hour round trip—they say Peter will be on the pier when we get back."

Gaunt went past them, out on the tiny balcony, and leaned his clenched fists on the rail, ignoring the view. Chillon was halfway to Carl Phillipe's boatyard—and by using the same departure time, by having the Corrans do the driving, he must hope to surprise any watch Henry Boisson was keeping on the hotel garage.

"Mr. Gaunt—" Maggie Corran was on her feet and tugging his sleeve. It was as if she'd read his mind. "What did they put in our car? Why does it matter so much?"

"Money," he said quietly. "Cut the bodywork open, and the reckoning is you'd find up to a half million pounds in smuggled currency."

Her eyes widened and her mouth shaped a shocked disbelief. Behind them, Frank Corran sat down on the edge of Anna's bed with a stunned expression.

Maggie Corran recovered first. "Then—then won't this man Boisson have people watching us?"

"He has, ever since you left home," said Gaunt. "You even know them—Hubbard and Dawson." He gave a slight, understanding smile and saved her the next question. "Yes, if they see you're not going to Boisson's garage they'll try to stop you. Except that the people who have Peter will be expecting that too. They'll be ready to deal with them."

"The way they've done before with others," said Anna bitterly from the background.

He nodded, brought Maggie Corran back into the room, and faced husband and wife.

"There's a chance I can get Peter out first," he said, then stopped their protest. "I said a chance—but if there's any risk to him, I won't try it. But if I get Peter out, then I expect something from you."

He saw them exchange a bewildered glance. Then Corran got to his feet, squeezed his wife's hand, and gave a slow, resolute nod.

"Just name it," he invited, his young face suddenly determined. "And—and I'm coming with you to get Peter."

"No chance," Gaunt answered. "You and Maggie daren't show your noses outside the Julien before noon." Turning, he was in time to forestall the other volunteer he'd expected. "You stay too, Anna—to keep an eye on them."

She gave him a glare, which grew even frostier when he winked at her.

"I still said name it," said Corran. "What do you want us to do—afterwards, I mean?"

"I'll tell you." Gaunt appreciated the optimism, which was more than his own. "Deliver the car to Automobiles Tamboure exactly the way Boisson ordered."

"You mean it?" Corran stared at him.

"Yes." He left it at that and went over to the telephone. "Now I'm going to organise some help my own way."

He dialed Sara Duffrey's number, praying to himself it wouldn't be engaged again, drawing a quick breath of relief as it rang out and was answered. In another moment Sara Duffrey was on the line—but in an irate mood.

"At last!" she snapped over the line with a heavy sarcasm. "Where are you? I've been trying to find you by 'phone for the last half hour."

"I've had problems."

"Now you've more, *mon ami*," she said tartly. "The girl Janine—Boisson's lady friend—is dead."

Gaunt winced. "How?"

"Killed by a car outside her apartment as she left for work this morning." Sara Duffrey paused to let it sink in. "Would you like to guess why the car didn't stop? That damned Boisson must have found out—"

"No," he cut her short heavily. "He didn't just find out. He knew, and he used her first. Her other friends took the wrong car last night. The one they want is the Corrans' station wagon—and right now it looks like they're going to get it."

He told her the rest in a few short sentences and at the end Sara Duffrey swore briefly but eloquently in a combination of three languages.

"What will you do?" she asked.

"Try the boatyard the way I did before," said Gaunt unemotionally. "But I'd like to know there's some back-up outside, just in case. I need someone here too, at the Julien, to help Anna."

"Your Mrs. Hart?" Sara Duffrey managed a chuckle. "*D'accord*. . . . Willi will be outside the boatyard in half an hour, I'll come to the Julien now. Will that do?"

"For starters," agreed Gaunt and hung up.

CHAPTER 7

Ten minutes later Jonathan Gaunt drove out of the cool gloom of the Hotel Julien's garage into the bright Montreux sunlight, reached the first road junction, and turned towards the centre of town, away from the lakeside route.

He drove quietly, keeping the Chrysler at a sedate pace through the traffic. If he was right, two sets of watchers were likely to have the hotel under observation—and he wanted to make sure he was clear of both. For a few minutes he steered a deliberate, casual course through the streets, keeping a constant eye on the rear-view mirror. Then, at last, satisfied, he turned the car again for the lakeside.

Gaunt drove in his shirt-sleeves, his jacket lying on the front passenger seat covering the Mauser pistol. His pace stayed unhurried. More than ninety minutes remained before the deadline for the Corrans came round—and in much less time than that the first issue would have been decided, one way or another.

It had become a familiar journey. First the cog railway passed by, then Chillon Castle. The sun reflected brightly from the white, quartz-veined rocks along the roadside and he passed a group of energetic, sweating cyclists who were toiling on in the heat, stripped to the waist.

The white fencing of the boatyard appeared ahead after

another few kilometres. A squad of men with a panel truck were repainting the road markings beside it and he had to slow as he passed them. It gave him the chance to see that the yard gate was firmly closed.

In another two minutes he stopped the Chrysler in the same snack-bar parking lot he'd used before. The sandy stretch of lakeside already had its quota of visitors sunning or playing along the water's edge, but this time he had no intention of joining the swimmers. He took another look at the fence. It ran down to the water's edge, then continued for a little distance as a low, half-submerged stone wall topped by barbed wire.

Leaving the car, carrying his jacket in a way that concealed the Mauser now in his waistband, he strolled through the family groups on the beach, reached the high fence, nodded cheerfully to a young couple who had settled in its shade, and walked casually towards the lapping water. The stonework beyond the fence was old and worn, the barbed wire rusty, and getting along and round it meant only a quick scramble. Another few moments and he was inside the yard, had dropped down on dry land again, and was crouching in the shelter of an old, up-turned dinghy.

Apart from the fact that the door of the office hut was lying open, little seemed to have changed. There was no-one in sight, the same old Volkswagen was parked outside the office, and the white ambulance was again lying inside the nearest of the open sheds.

Then, still crouching low, Gaunt spotted something that was different. Behind the ambulance lay another, lower shape covered by a large tarpaulin.

It was time to find out how long his luck would hold.

Abandoning his jacket, he drew the Mauser, slipped the safety catch, and began to work his way nearer. A low stack of timber gave him cover part of the way, he moved from there to a clutter of empty, abandoned oil drums, then had to make a quick, padding dash across a short final 'stretch which was in full view of the office window.

As he reached the shed he heard a telephone begin ringing in the office. Dropping down beside the ambulance, he saw a man move across the window, then the telephone was answered.

The radiator of the ambulance still felt warm to the touch. Cautiously, on his feet again, Gaunt went deeper into the shed to the canvas-shrouded shape at the rear. A trolley beside it held gas cylinders and an oxy-acetylene cutting outfit and he knew what he was going to find even before he lifted an edge of the tarpaulin.

James and Mary Walker wouldn't have been happy to see their green Ford coupe. It was on a ramp and the metal bodywork had been cut open in several places as if attacked by a maniac with a giant tin-opener.

A humourless grin touched Gaunt's lips. But he quickly lowered the tarpaulin again and huddled into the shadows of a stack of wooden battens at the rear of the mangled car as footsteps came crunching towards the shed.

The stockily built man with his arm in a sling came in. He went straight to the ambulance, unlocked the rear door, and looked inside. Giving a satisfied grunt, he locked the door again, turned, and left.

Gaunt waited until the footsteps had crunched back across the yard. Then he went over to the ambulance, swore softly as he discovered the front doors were also locked, and had to settle for pressing his nose against one of the side windows, peering in.

The bunks were empty. But a small figure lay curled on the floor between them, apparently asleep.

He'd found Peter Corran—after literally walking past him. But now he had to decide what came next. He stood for a moment, half-listening to the sound of the traffic outside the yard, then the louder, vibrating rumble of a passing heavy truck gave him an idea.

There were some rags lying beside the oxy-acetylene gear. He used them to pad the Mauser's butt, then waited patiently beside one of the rear windows until he heard another truck rumbling along. As the noise reached its peak, he slammed the padded pistol-butt against the glass, winced at the way the glass still shattered, then crouched tensely beside the ambulance with the butt of the pistol in his grasp again and his finger on the trigger.

Nothing happened. He drew a breath of relief, put his free hand through the hole in the glass, felt for the interior door catch—then almost yelped at the unexpected pain as a set of sharp young teeth sank into his wrist.

"Cut it out, Peter," he said in an agonised whisper. "I'm a friend of your dad—you know me."

The bite ended and he heard a sniffle. Wrist stinging, Gaunt found the door catch, opened the door, and grinned at the small, tearful face staring up at him.

"Remember me?" he asked softly.

Peter Corran nodded cautiously.

"Right. Stay quiet and we'll be on our way back to the hotel very soon. Okay?"

"In time for lunch?" asked the small boy gravely. "I'm hungry. Want lunch."

"In time for lunch," agreed Gaunt, rubbing his wrist. "No need to turn cannibal. Now, stay put for a moment."

He lifted Peter onto one of the bunks and squeezed forward to the driver's seat. As he'd expected, the Citroen had a steering-column lock. But he pulled the wiring harness out from under the dashboard and scowled at it for a moment. Then, bringing out his pocket-knife, he quickly cut and bared a couple of wires. When he was finished, he was almost certain he'd by-passed the ignition cut-off for the horn.

"Right, laddie." He lifted Peter Corran forward and set him in the driver's seat. The child's head hardly reached above the centre of the steering wheel as Gaunt pointed to the horn button. "I want you to sound the horn for me. You know how to do that? No"—he stopped the small fingers just in time—"not yet. But when I'm outside and wave to you. Then just keep blowing it. Understand, Peter?"

"Yes." Tears forgotten, the young face grinned with excited delight. "Then lunch?"

"Then lunch," promised Gaunt, and hoped he was right. "But don't start that horn till I wave. Remember that, Peter."

Going to the back of the shed, Gaunt selected one of the shorter lengths of timber from the stack of thick wooden battens. Then he moved forward again, positioning himself against the shed wall close to the open front and near to the ambulance and the small, expectant figure behind the wheel. Switching the batten to his right hand, clutching the Mauser in his left, he checked his position again, then waved.

The horn blasted, the note wavering for a moment, then

settling into a long, piercing bray which was almost deafening inside the hut's confines. He could see Peter beaming from ear to ear as the four-year-old kept the button jammed down.

Seconds later a stocky, angry figure charged into the hut. It was the man with the sling again, heading straight for the driver's door with the key in his good hand—and as he passed, Gaunt took one step out from the shadows.

The wooden batten swung in a flat, fast arc and connected with the hi-jacker's head, giving a sound like a muffled drum-beat while the force vibrated back to Gaunt's wrist. The man pitched forward, sheer impetus sending him skidding along the dirt floor until he came to rest, motionless and face down.

Tossing the batten aside, Gaunt quickly switched the Mauser to his right hand. The horn's sound had begun to waver, as if Peter Corran was becoming tired of the "game" but it was still enough.

Long-jawed face contorted with rage, Carl Phillipe came running in—then skidded to an alarmed halt as he saw the unconscious figure on the floor and tried to swing round, one hand snaking towards his hip. But he froze, his cold blue eyes widening as they took in the way the Mauser's muzzle was trained on his middle.

Then he shrugged and, without waiting for any order, his hands came up well clear of his body.

Keeping the man covered, Gaunt crossed to the ambulance, opened the door, and gently removed Peter Corran's hand from the horn.

"Any more of you?" he asked.

Carefully and precisely, Carl Phillipe spat on the ground

near his feet. A chuckle of dry amusement came from the hut entrance and Gaunt glanced round—then relaxed.

It was Willi Fanton, and his leathery face held a grin of open admiration as he considered the scene, hands stuffed in his trouser pockets.

"*Félicitations*, M'sieu Gaunt," he said, coming forward. "You told my sister you needed back-up, but right now I'm not sure why. Now, if you could get our friend here to turn round—"

Gaunt nodded to Carl Phillipe, who scowled but obeyed. Swiftly, with a practised ease, Willi Fanton frisked the man and collected a gun from a hip holster. There was a soft clink of metal—and when Fanton stepped back the mousey-haired hi-jacker wore handcuffs.

"Much better," mused Fanton. He winked at Peter Corran, who was watching wide-eyed from the ambulance, stooped over the man on the ground, and repeated the performance. This time he collected a long-bladed knife from a leg-sheath before he glanced round. "Ah—to answer your question, these two are all the rats in this particular trap."

Gaunt heard footsteps outside, then voices. Puzzled, he took a few steps forward and looked out into the boatyard. Several men were moving round it, some wearing paint-smeared overalls—and the yard gate lay wide open. He turned, to find Willi Fanton eyeing him apologetically, and suddenly remembered the road-marking squad he'd seen outside the yard.

"Just who the hell are you, Willi?" he asked with a tight suspicion.

"Police—an *inspecteur* in the companies investigation section," said Fanton with a degree of embarrassment. He gave a slight warning frown and thumbed in Carl Phillipe's direction. "Maybe I can explain one or two things later, eh?"

"It would be an idea," agreed Gaunt.

Fanton showed his teeth in a smile. "When we heard the car horn, it seemed a good time to move in. And now, if we get things a little tidier here—"

He went out into the yard, shouted an order, and came back with three of his men. Grinning, one lifted Peter Corran out of the ambulance, hoisted him on one shoulder, and ambled off. At a nod from Fanton the other two unceremoniously rolled the unconscious hi-jacker onto his back.

"That one I think I know," murmured Fanton. "But it can wait."

Another nod and the two carried the limp figure out of the shed like a sack of grain. While they did, Fanton strolled to the rear of the shed, lifted the tarpaulin covering the Walkers' car, looked at it for a moment, grimaced, then came back.

"*Eh bien*, so what are we left with?" He rubbed a hand across his bald pate and considered the handcuffed Carl Phillipe grimly. "Everything from malicious damage through extortion to murder. My sergeant will need a new ribbon for his typewriter when he starts sorting this lot out."

Carl Phillipe's long-jawed face twisted and the man swore at them curtly and unemotionally. Shaping a small grin, Fanton shrugged at Gaunt.

"We have proof for some, we can work on the rest," he said dryly, then faced Carl Phillipe again. "I want the little friend you still have on the loose—somewhere near the Hotel Julien, I think. Where do we collect him?"

"*Pardon* . . . I've forgotten," said the man cynically. "Find out."

"Janine is dead," said Willi Fanton quietly. He saw the total disbelief that flared in the cold blue eyes and nodded. "It's the truth."

"How?" asked the man.

"A car, outside her apartment two hours ago." Fanton paused, then added softly and deliberately, "The driver didn't stop. Would you like to guess why?"

"Boisson." It came like a sigh. For a long moment he stood as if carved from stone, then he stirred, the handcuff links jingling, and glared at them. "Well, was it Boisson?"

"We think so," said Fanton, his leathery face impassive. "*Mais oui* . . . we think. But proving it may be different. It was a stolen car and we found it later—empty. You understand?"

Slowly, bitterly, the man nodded.

"She was working for me," he said in a dull, toneless voice. "More than that—and for a long time—"

"And last night she tipped you that the Walkers' car was the one with the money?" suggested Gaunt.

"She 'phoned, once Boisson left her," agreed Carl Phillipe. He scowled at Gaunt. "And she said Boisson was having you killed—that he reckoned you were one of my people. He had the notion you were travelling with the Safari as another way of trying to spot the money car."

"Maybe he got it half right," said Gaunt. He glanced at Fanton, who nodded for him to go on. "So how did you feel when you discovered Janine had been fooled—that you'd got the wrong car?"

"How do you think? I contacted Janine, told her if there was even one more hint Boisson suspected her she was to get out—get out fast." The blue eyes hooded for a moment. "She shouldn't have waited."

"She helped you hi-jack the last two shipments?"

"You know about them?" Carl Phillipe showed surprise, then straightened a little, scuffed a foot along the dirt floor, and nodded. "In the beginning, it was Janine's idea—and we had Boisson almost driven mad."

"But not this time." Grimly, Willi Fanton picked up the questioning again. "He fooled you into stealing the Walkers' car. After that, what made you so sure the shipment had to be in the Corrans' Ford?"

Carl Phillipe sighed wearily. "Janine knew the shipment had been arranged weeks ago, and that Boisson's escort in the Saab didn't have it—"

"But you still tried to knock out the Saab along the way," interrupted Gaunt, frowning.

"You remember a man killed beside a fairground in France?" asked the hi-jacker in the same hoarse voice. "He was one of my people. They killed him—left him dying anyway. Is it my fault a fool of a truck driver made a mistake and got the wrong car that day?"

"A mistake." Disgust and contempt showed on Willi Fanton's face. "I asked you about the Corran family. Why them, after the Walkers?"

"Because to the outsider they were the most unlikely of all, and Boisson's mind works that way," said Carl Phillipe.

"More important, we knew they and the Walkers were the first people to book on this Safari. And who else was left? Him?" He glared bleakly in Gaunt's direction. "The girl with the sports car? Those two old schoolteachers?"

Willi Fanton stood silent for a moment, then looked round. One of his men was hovering near and he signalled him over.

"Take him," said Fanton dryly. "Get the rest from him —the Hotel Julien arrangements." He looked straight at Carl Phillipe for a moment. "That'll help too, if we're going to settle with Boisson."

The hi-jacker gave a slight nod, then was led away. Sighing, Willi Fanton leaned back against the ambulance, brought out his cigarettes, put one between his lips and tossed another to Gaunt. Silently, they shared the flame of Gaunt's lighter.

"*C'est ça* . . . the first part anyway," mused Fanton, drawing on his cigarette. He let the smoke trickle out slowly, watching Gaunt. "You know, it was only a small deception—a policeman is just another kind of civil servant."

"But I don't like being used," said Gaunt grimly.

"Used?" Fanton winced at the word. "You have it wrong. The arrangement I have with your Henry Falconer in Edinburgh is a completely unofficial one—and it works both ways."

"You scratch my back, I'll get someone to scratch yours?" suggested Gaunt with a frosty politeness.

Fanton chuckled. "M'sieu Gaunt, when I am not officially involved in something I have a poor memory—like for a certain incident at Chillon you told me about last night. So—ah—if there was deception, can't we say it was in a good cause?"

"Go to hell," said Gaunt wryly, then had to grin. "All right, I'm not arguing."

"*Bon.*" Fanton drew on his cigarette again, then became serious. "Which leaves Henry Boisson—whom we both want, for different reasons. But I still need proof he killed that girl—and your currency offences have no standing here, except as evidence."

"The delivery is at noon," said Gaunt, and glanced at his watch. There was just under an hour to go.

"And before that, we have a certain young man to return to his parents, eh?" Willi Fanton heaved himself upright, tossed his cigarette away, and smiled. "Then, as my sister might say, maybe we're both due a dividend."

When they went out, a patrol van was just leaving the boatyard with its two prisoners aboard. Fanton went over to the office, talked to one of his men who was standing by the door, and came back looking pleased.

"We'll send the boy on ahead, I think," he decided. "My sergeant can smuggle him into the Hotel Julien through one of the rear doors and get him back to his parents. We—ah—have another little job to do first."

"Like what?" Gaunt raised an eyebrow.

"Your third man. His friends say he is waiting with a laundry truck near the hotel. If Corran is followed when he leaves, then—" Fanton smacked his hands together. "Or that was the plan."

Minutes later, Willi Fanton beside him in the passenger

seat and an unmarked police car close behind, Jonathan Gaunt was back behind the wheel of his own car again, driving towards Montreux. At exactly eleven-thirty they turned into a side street near the hotel and he drew into the kerb and halted as Fanton touched his arm. Glancing in the rear-view mirror, he saw the police car coasting in to stop behind them.

The laundry truck was a stone's throw ahead, parked near the corner so that the driver had a view of the hotel garage entrance—and what happened next was smooth and simple.

Two plain-clothes men left the police car, ambled down the road together, reached the van, suddenly wrenched open its door, and dived inside. They emerged again in a moment with Carl Phillipe's dark, sharp-faced "ambulance driver" between them. The police car purred forward, the prisoner was bundled aboard, and it drove away.

"One less detail to worry about," murmured Fanton. "Shall we go?"

They used another little maze of side streets to reach the service entry behind the Hotel Julien, parked there, and got out. Willi Fanton's sergeant was standing at the service door, a grin on his face.

"The reunion *joyeuse* is over," said Willi Fanton with a touch of relief after a few words with the man. "It should be safe enough to go up."

They used the service elevator, arrived beside the seventh-floor fire stairway, exchanged nods with another of Fanton's men, and arrived at Anna Hart's room. The door was lying open but the only person inside was Sara Duffrey, who was sprawled back in a chair reading a financial magazine. She nodded to her brother, then turned her head, called towards the balcony, and Anna came through.

"You're all right?" she asked Gaunt simply.

He nodded. "How's the boy?"

"Hungry." She gave a slight, incredulous smile. "Maggie has him next door, eating his way through about a year's supply of sausages. It—well, you should have seen how they were, when they got him back."

"A child of that age I would have paid to have taken away again," murmured Sara Duffrey with a mock scowl. She got up and glanced at her brother. "M'sieu Corran now?"

Willi Fanton gave a grunt of agreement. She went out and returned in a moment with Frank Corran, who stopped when he saw Gaunt, moistened his lips, and started to stammer his thanks.

"Forget that," said Gaunt with a curtness which halted Corran almost before he'd begun. "You've a job to do— and it's the only reason stopping me from beating the hell out of you right here and now."

Corran flushed. There was a sudden silence in the little room, intensified by the low background murmur of traffic from outside.

"Look, I"—Corran licked his lips—"all right, I was a fool to get into this, but—"

"You took your wife and child into it too," said Gaunt stonily. He thought of the man dying on the cobbles outside a French hotel, of the elderly couple dragged from their wrecked holiday car, all the rest of the last few days.

"They're alive—they're the lucky ones. But next time, try

sticking their heads in a gas oven. The odds are about as good."

Anna had a frown on her face, but said nothing. Sara Duffrey lit one of her thin cheroots and gave a slight shrug, a mere interested spectator. Only Willi Fanton voiced any reaction.

"But I am sure if M'sieu Corran now assists us—" he began heavily.

"He will," said Gaunt grimly, cutting him short. "He'll do the delivery exactly as Boisson told him, no more, no less. Because that's the only way he's going to keep himself outside a prison cell for the next few years." Deliberately, he glanced at his watch. "You leave in fifteen minutes."

Frank Corran swallowed hard, looked at the others, then turned on his heel and went out.

"Jonny," said Anna in a tight voice. "What on earth was that all about? I mean, he—" She stopped there, bewildered.

"He is one very lucky young man," mused Sara Duffrey with a wise, approving smile. "But now he has had what you might call the hell scared out of him. It is the right mood for what he has to do."

Gaunt hadn't seen it that way. But he didn't argue—explaining would have taken too long. All he knew was there had been a moment when he'd had to hold his hands tight at his side to stop them shaking, to stop him hitting Frank Corran.

The Chrysler had been standing in the direct glare of the sun and the seats were hot, the steering wheel almost pain-

ful to the touch. It was a couple of minutes before noon
and Gaunt was behind the wheel, waiting where the laundry truck had been before. Willi Fanton was beside him,
nursing a small two-way radio between his hands, his face
impassive.

The Swiss had three police cars deployed in the area,
though Gaunt didn't know where and their existence came
down to the occasional murmur of a voice over the radio.
Eyes half closed against the glare, he watched the Hotel
Julien's garage entrance and felt his patience draining away
as the seconds ticked by.

Then, exactly on time, Frank Corran's yellow Ford station wagon drove out, hesitated as it reached the road, and
slipped into the traffic stream. A moment later, as the car
passed, they had a glimpse of the slight fair-haired driver
sitting tensely behind the wheel—and Willi Fanton
grunted.

Already Corran had company. The blue Saab, with Hubbard and Dawson aboard, nosed out of a line of parked vehicles almost opposite the hotel and tucked in behind the
Ford. It was no surprise. The Saab had been under police
observation for several minutes.

Gaunt let them go. Another full minute passed before
he exchanged a glance with Fanton, started the Chrysler,
and set it moving.

The radio murmured on every now and again as they
drove. The three unmarked police cars were carrying out a
standard pattern surveillance—each taking a turn of tailing,
none waiting long enough in that role to be spotted. And it
was an easy enough task. Frank Corran was heading

directly for the Automobiles Tamboure garage and the blue Saab was cruising a gentle few car-lengths behind.

The Chrysler was still some distance away when the radio spoke again, a short, crisp message which brought a satisfied smile to Willi Fanton's lips.

Corran had arrived at the garage and had driven the Ford into the workshop. Hubbard and Dawson had stopped their car in the forecourt and had also gone into the garage. A little later, as Gaunt pulled into the kerb near the tip of the T-junction street, the Saab was still lying empty in the forecourt ahead, and everything looked totally peaceful and ordinary.

They had hardly settled down to wait when Frank Corran walked out of the garage building, crossed the road ahead, and came down the narrow street towards them. As he drew level, Willi Fanton reached back, opened the rear door, and closed it again as the man got in.

"Well?" demanded Gaunt without looking round.

"Like you wanted, no problems—none I know about anyway." Corran fumbled for his cigarettes and lit one clumsily. "I just handed over the car to a mechanic, said it was booked in." He drew hard on the cigarette, trembling a little. "Boisson's there. He just grinned at me, didn't say anything. Like I said, no problems."

"If there had been, do you think you'd have walked out of there again?" asked Gaunt grimly. "Did you see Hubbard and Dawson?"

Corran nodded. "They talked to me as I left. Hubbard said their car was having brake-fade trouble—they wanted someone to have a look at it."

"As long as you looked as though you believed them," murmured Willi Fanton. "*Merci* . . . now get back to your hotel and stay there." He paused. "And that, M'sieu Corran, is an order."

The man left them, walking quickly down the street and not glancing back. As he vanished, Willi Fanton settled down again with a sigh.

"Now we're the people with a problem," said Gaunt dryly, guessing what was troubling him. "How long do we wait?"

Shrugging, Fanton scowled towards the garage. "You know what I want."

"Boisson holding a sack of money in his hot little hand," said Gaunt. He had been making his own calculation. "I'd give them half an hour to open up the car."

Willi Fanton reacted cautiously and wanted an hour. They tossed a coin for it at last and the half hour won. The rest of the plan was simple enough—one police car's crew detailed to watch the rear of the garage, the remaining two cars to follow Gaunt and Fanton straight in.

The half hour passed with an agonising slowness in the mid-day heat. Housewives shopped up and down the street, an occasional customer came and went at the garage ahead. Now and again the radio in Fanton's lap muttered briefly and he answered, but the rest of the time he sat whistling tunelessly through his teeth until Gaunt thought the sound would drive him mad.

It came as a relief when the last few seconds had ticked away. Glancing at his passenger, Gaunt drew a small smile and a nod, then leaned forward to start the engine while Fanton used the radio briefly.

The Chrysler drew away from the kerb, purred up to the head of the T junction, paused briefly for a gap in the traffic—then Gaunt slammed his foot on the accelerator and the car answered with a snarling rasp of power and a scream of tyre rubber.

They crossed the road, screeched a way through the forecourt area, and went straight through the big, open doors into the workshop area. Behind them, the two police cars had materialised and were skidding to a halt, blocking the forecourt, their crews tumbling out—but Gaunt's impression, as he broadsided the Chrysler to a halt in the middle of the workshop, was of open-mouthed, wide-eyed mechanics and of a balding figure staring from just outside an office door.

It was Tom Hubbard. The bulky Englishman's surprise lasted only a moment, then he was diving for the shelter of a workbench with a gun in his hand.

The first bullet smashed one of the Chrysler's headlamps. Wrenching the steering wheel round, accelerating again, Gaunt rammed the workbench as a second shot hit the car. The bench and Hubbard were thrown aside by the impact and the man lay still, trapped under its wreckage.

They had hardly stopped as Willi Fanton tumbled out of the passenger side, a gun in his hand. Gaunt followed, saw a new figure dart out of the office doorway and start to run—then gave a quick grin as Eric Dawson halted again at the sight of the line of armed police coming in from the forecourt. White-faced, Dawson raised his hands in surrender and was prodded back the way he'd come by a Swiss plain-clothes man's machine-pistol.

A noisy compressor was thudding away in the background, drowning almost everything else as Fanton's men began herding the garage staff into a small, bewildered group. Fanton stopped briefly beside Hubbard, who was still lying where he'd fallen, then rose and glared round anxiously.

"He'll live," he told Gaunt, shouting above the compressor's din. "But where's Boisson—and that damned car?"

Neither were in sight. Grabbing Eric Dawson by the shirt-front, Gaunt hauled him close.

"Where's Boisson?" he demanded.

The thin, sallow Scot hesitated, then yelped as Willi Fanton gave him a back-handed cuff across the face.

"Out there, through the back—" Dawson gestured fearfully towards a metal door at the rear of the workshop. "He took Corran's car through to the bodyshop—"

Heaving Dawson back into the grasp of one of the plain-clothes men, Gaunt drew his Mauser and followed Fanton at a run to a tracked iron door at the back of the workshop. A yank on a pulley-chain heaved it open wide enough for them to get through. Two policemen carrying machine-pistols following them, they emerged in a small, cobbled courtyard surrounded by a wall. The sides of the courtyard were lined with accident-damaged or partly repaired vehicles and in the middle was a large, flat-roofed brick workshop.

The main workshop door was closed. Willi Fanton tried the handle of the small access door set beside it, stepped back, and nodded to the nearest of his men.

A heavy, booted foot kicked the edge of the door with a

piston-like force, connecting just below the lock—and the locked door burst open, banging back on its hinges as they poured through.

Next in after Fanton, Jonathan Gaunt saw Frank Corran's yellow station wagon up on a ramp in the middle of the big, brightly lit bodyshop. Its tail was towards them, the only two figures in the bodyshop were beside it, staring round at them—Henry Boisson and a man wearing a welder's face-helmet who had been using an oxy-acetylene burner, its nozzle still tipped with hissing flame.

A section of the station wagon's tail had been cut away near one wheel arch and the burner had almost completed doing the same at the other. An open suitcase at Boisson's feet already held several small, plastic-wrapped bundles and another one was in his hands.

Both men had swung round to stare at the eruption through the door, Boisson letting the package fall and clawing for his pocket.

"Police," yelled Willi Fanton—and the gun that had appeared in Boisson's hand spat an answer.

The bullet slammed into Fanton's shoulder, throwing the heavily built Swiss against Gaunt, momentarily blocking the two plain-clothes police still following them in. Firing a wild shot, Boisson shoved his companion aside, knocking the sputtering burner from his grip.

Then Boisson turned to run, and there was a side door none of them had noticed till then on the far side of the bodyshop. Willi Fanton was cursing, Gaunt was bringing up his Mauser for a two-handed shot—but the machine-pistol held by the plain-clothes man beside Fanton snarled first.

It was a short, stitching burst which hurled Boisson back

against the Ford's mangled tail-gate, and while it still echoed Boisson first tried to hold on to the tail-gate, then fell to his knees. But the scream of terror that came from the man who had been using the burner was for another reason.

A gush of fuel was jetting from the station wagon's tank, where a bullet had pierced it. The liquid splashed on the concrete, near the burner's gas-fed flame, there was a searing flash, and an instant later the vehicle's tank exploded in a white-heat blast.

Gaunt had a momentary, horrifying view of Boisson and his companion as they died in the centre of the fireball's fury. Then, like the others, he cowered down as debris rained round them like shrapnel while windows shattered and the heat scorched over them.

It was an hour later when the two charred bodies were brought out of the wrecked building, where a twisted heap of burned-out metal was all that remained of the yellow station wagon.

There were fire engines and ambulances in the garage forecourt and uniformed police seemed everywhere. Standing in the middle of it, Willi Fanton watched the stretchers with their plastic-sheeted loads being put aboard one of the ambulances. His shoulder was bandaged, a piece of sticking plaster covered a cut on his bald head, and he sighed as he turned to Gaunt.

"I didn't want it this way," he said in a weary voice. "*Mais non . . .* and that other poor devil who was with him—"

"It happened," said Gaunt grimly, that one picture of the men in the fireball still not shaken from his mind. "It happened, you couldn't help it—and you've got your proof."

Hubbard and Dawson were talking, so were a few of the garage staff who had been on the fringe of Boisson's operation. Gaunt's mouth twisted at another thought. About the only thing they didn't have was the currency that had been in Corran's car. Only a few burned fragments of notes and some stirred-up ash had remained by the time the fire was out.

"All that's left is to sort it out," agreed Willi Fanton almost sadly.

He stopped there as they had to move aside to let a fireman pass, rolling up a hose-line. Then, deliberately, he walked the few paces to where Gaunt's car was lying and considered the damaged front end.

"A new headlamp and some small, temporary repairs and it could be driven," he said. "You agree?"

"Yes." Something in Willi Fanton's voice made Gaunt raise an eyebrow. "Am I going anywhere?"

"I think so," said Fanton slowly, his eyes apologetic. "I want you out of Switzerland before midnight. A lot of things would be simpler that way—reports, explanations, all the rest of it. You understand?"

"Like suddenly I'm an embarrassment?"

"To your people and mine," agreed Fanton sadly. "I agree it is wrong, crazy maybe."

"But that's how it goes." Gaunt nodded and mentally damned all officialdom. "So let's get the car fixed."

It was nearing dusk when Gaunt drove out of Montreux with a parting gift from Willi Fanton, a bottle of brandy, jammed into the dashboard compartment. The setting sun was glinting on Lake Geneva, the mountains in the distance had taken on a soft red hue, and all he could do about it was curse.

Though he had a few final memories. A wry grin crossed his face as he kept up with the flow of traffic on the broad autoroute.

The Montreux police department garage had replaced the Chrysler's headlamp and the other temporary repairs free of charge—then he'd been more or less escorted back to the Hotel Julien to check out.

He hadn't seen the Corrans. They'd been taken away by Willi Fanton's men for more questions—though with a promise that that would be the end of it. It didn't matter that Mary Walker and her husband had ignored him, far too busy creating hell about their damaged car and the insurance claim to bother about anything else.

Mrs. MacLean and Miss Stewart had made up for that. The two retired schoolteachers had been oddly upset when they'd heard he was leaving because of "a business problem back home."

"We were going to take you to the casino," Miss Stewart had complained.

To play blackjack, where they'd worked out a system. It was, in their opinion, more intellectual than horse races and they had their first day's winnings to prove it.

Which had left Sara Duffrey and Anna.

He shrugged a little to himself, letting a big silver-grey Rolls Royce surge past. Sara Duffrey had given him the bad news first, that all dealings in Rhuvalla shares had been suspended and the liquidator had moved in. There was going to be no magic wand in that direction.

Then, as she'd given him a farewell embrace like a bear-hug, she'd had a quick, final murmur in his ear, one that still puzzled him.

"Safe journey, Jonny, and don't worry if you're delayed." She'd given a soft chuckle. "Your Henry Falconer has always been *sympathique* when I ask a favour, like I'm going to do."

Gaunt could believe it and he wasn't going to ask why.

And that had only left Anna Hart, who had puzzled him too. She'd come out to the car to say good-bye, but it had been an oddly cool farewell—not much more than a brush of her lips against his and an almost withdrawn smile.

He left the autoroute at the next turn-off and soon the road began winding and climbing towards the mountains which marked the French frontier. As he drove on, both hands resting lightly on the steering wheel's rim, Gaunt glanced briefly at the package lying beside him.

It had been Willi Fanton's other gift, a photocopy of the money-laundry records his men had found in Henry Boisson's office safe. A lot of people back in Britain were going to be very busy when that lot landed on their desks.

Dusk was beginning to grey in across the landscape. Another car's lights showed in his driving mirror, coming up fast, handled well.

Gaunt glanced at it again, then a third time—and braked hard.

The little sports car flashed its lights and kept coming. He grinned, knowing now what Sara Duffrey had meant.

So his bank balance had gone to hell, his car was dented, the Rhuvalla shares were a disaster.

There were other priorities.

He pulled in at the side of the road and waited for Anna Hart to catch up.